ZEROED IN

ZEROED IN

THE SILENCER SERIES BOOK 12

MIKE RYAN

WWW.MIKERYANBOOKS.COM

1

A month had passed since the takeover of the hospital by The Scorpions. Things around the city had been pretty quiet since then, at least as far as that group was concerned. Recker and Haley were still pretty busy doing their usual thing, though everything was pretty easy according to their standards. The Scorpions had gone into hiding, having to regroup after losing a couple of their top guys. Though the hope throughout the city was that they had left, licking their wounds after realizing they couldn't run over everyone in their way, Recker and the gang knew better. It was only a matter of time before they reappeared again. And they would likely be just as lethal and violent as before. Maybe even more so, thinking that they needed to be even tougher and badder than ever to survive.

Recker had just gotten to the office, taking most of

the morning off. It was Mia's return to work, and he wanted to make sure she was up for it before she left. She was actually ready to go back a week before that, but Recker was successful in convincing her to take the extra time. He had more fears about her going back than she did. He was worried about something bad happening again, even though he knew what happened the previous month was a once in a lifetime type of event. Mia wasn't that worried herself. She knew what happened would probably never happen again. She didn't have any fears about going back. But the worry was still evident across Recker's face as he walked by his friends.

"Everything will be fine," Jones said.

"What?"

"Mia will be fine."

"Who said she wouldn't?"

"Your face says so. I can see it written across it."

"I'm not worried," Recker said.

"Uh, huh. So that's why you took the morning off? So that's why you have that look on your face? Because you're not worried?"

"I took the morning off because it was her first day back at work. It had nothing to do with me being worried."

"Oh, OK."

"Instead of analyzing me, how about we talk about what's going on?"

Jones looked perplexed. He wasn't aware of

anything happening at the moment. "Going on? What's going on?"

"I dunno. I assume something is. Isn't there usually something?"

"Usually so. But not at the moment."

"Oh." Recker looked around the office, noticing the absence of one of his partners. "So where's Chris?"

"Out."

"Doing what?"

"He had an assignment."

"You just told me nothing was happening."

"I said there's nothing happening at the moment. And there is not."

"But you just said Chris was on an assignment."

"He was. He's not now."

"You just said…"

"I said he *was* on an assignment. That job has been completed. He's on his way back to the office now. So therefore, since we have no other jobs to do at the present time, nothing is happening, and nothing is going on. See how that works?"

"Oh, you're being a wiseguy now?"

"Well I have to take something from you, don't I?"

"You just type away there. Leave the humor to me."

"So how is Mia, anyway? Ready to go back to work?"

"She was ready to go back two weeks ago."

"She's a tough woman."

"She is. Hopefully she never goes through a situation like that again."

"Mike, the odds of a situation like that happened again to her are probably astronomical."

"I know. It's just... if it happens once, it can happen again."

"The only way I could see it happening again is if The Scorpions realize she's your girlfriend and deliberately try something because of that."

"I know. And that's what worries me."

"But they won't find that out."

"But what if they do?" Recker asked.

"How would they?"

Recker shrugged. "I don't know. How does anyone find anything out? Dig a little, loose lips, in the right spot at the right time, or the wrong spot for that matter. Just by mistake. Things like that happen."

"I don't think you have to worry about that."

"We'll see. How long until Chris gets back?"

Jones looked at the time. "Probably twenty minutes or so."

"What was he working on?"

"Domestic violence situation. A man texted his wife that he was going to kill her. They had been separated for the past month."

"He have any problems with it?"

"No. He had a little chat with the man and took care of it without a problem."

Another ten minutes went by, with Recker

checking out his gun cabinet to pass the time, making sure everything was cleaned and ready to go. His phone started ringing, and he instinctively thought it might have been Mia, having a problem about returning to work. He was surprised to see that it wasn't, and maybe a little happy too. Though upon seeing that it was Malloy, he knew something was probably up, and not for the better.

"Hey, what's up?"

"You know, the usual," Malloy replied.

"Something bad?"

"That's the usual, isn't it?"

"I suppose it is. So what's up now?"

"Vincent would like to chat with you."

"What for?"

"I dunno. Something about The Scorpions I think."

"They back?"

"Did they leave?"

"What else is up?"

"I don't know. I'm pretty sure it's just about The Scorpions. What exactly, or anything else, I'm not sure."

"What's going on with them?"

"I dunno. Boss just said he wanted to meet with you."

"When?"

"As soon as you can make it. Now would be ideal he said. But tomorrow would work too if you can't make it today."

"Uh, no, I can make it now. Where? Usual spot I take it?"

"You got it. It's lunchtime."

Recker laughed. "So it is."

"So I'll tell him you'll be there?"

"I'll be there."

"See you then."

After Recker hung up the phone, he stood next to his cabinet, just staring at the wall. His actions weren't lost on Jones, who could tell something was on his mind. There always was something when he did that.

"What was that about?" Jones asked.

"Vincent wants a meet."

"What for?"

"Something about The Scorpions."

"What about them?"

"I don't know. That's what he wants to talk about, apparently."

"And I take it you're going?"

"Don't I always?"

Jones let out a sigh. "Unfortunately yes. You always do."

"Doesn't it usually wind up being good that I do?"

"That's debatable."

"For who?"

"For us."

"Usually always get something out of it," Recker said.

"Yes, more headaches and more problems. If that is

what you are referring to, then yes, we most certainly get something out of it."

"I was talking about information."

"I guess sometimes we get that too."

"David, Vincent doesn't just call for a meeting to shoot the breeze. If he says it's something about The Scorpions, I gotta imagine it's pretty good and is worth our while."

"Perhaps."

"All I've got to lose is my time."

"Well, I wouldn't say that's all you've got to lose, but, I know you're going, so there's that."

"You make it sound like you're not interested in their whereabouts?"

"To be honest, I'd be quite happy if they moved on and we never heard about them again."

"We both know what the odds of that are," Recker said. "They're not going away. They're just regrouping. And when they reappear again... watch out. I have a feeling they're going to be worse than ever."

"Well there's something to look forward to. I was hoping that they would decide the effort to remain here is too great and they would move on for easier pastures somewhere else."

Recker shook his head. "Their pride is hurt now. Wounded. They won't, can't, admit defeat that easily. They can't let it get out that they were run out of some-where. Hurts their ego. And it makes it easier for others to stand up to them, thinking they're not as big and tough and bad as they've heard about. No, they can't leave. Not now."

Jones sighed. "So once again we are going to get sidetracked from our main objective to deal with some riff-raff that's going to take up most of our time."

"We both know that's the way it goes sometimes."

"Unfortunately yes. And it happens too often."

"All comes with the territory."

"Are you going to wait until Chris comes back?"

"No, I'll just head out now," Recker answered. "I don't need backup for Vincent. Just keep him on standby in case something develops while I'm gone."

"So I'll put him on speed dial is what you're saying."

Recker smirked. "Funny."

"And you say I never take any of your traits."

"What'd I tell you before? Leave the humor to me." Recker closed his gun cabinet, then got ready to leave. "Want me to call you on the way back?"

"Only if you have something interesting to tell me."

"Don't I always?"

"What did I tell you before? Unfortunately, yes."

"Funny man."

"I'm trying to spread my wings," Jones said.

"Well, don't spread them too far. Stick to what suits you best."

"So being a thorn in your side?"

Recker smiled as he walked out the door. "See you later, Professor."

2

After entering the building, Recker exchanged handshakes with Malloy. Recker looked him over, noticing that he didn't look the worse for wear.

"Doesn't even getting shot get you a vacation?"

Malloy smiled. "Who needs them? Aren't we already living in Paradise?"

"If this is Paradise, I'd hate to see your definition of Hell."

Malloy snickered. "Might be the same thing."

Recker nodded. "Might be at that."

Recker then walked down to the end of the restaurant, finding Vincent at his usual and favorite table. He had just ordered and given the menu back to the waitress as Recker sat down across from him.

"Not too late to get you something," Vincent said.

"I'm good, thanks."

Vincent smiled. "I always forget, you get that good home cooking."

"Not too much lately."

Vincent nodded. "How is she doing these days?"

"As good as can be expected. Going back to work."

"Good to hear. I'm glad for the both of you. She's a tough one."

"She is."

"I wouldn't expect anything less from a girlfriend of yours."

"Well, I can't really take any credit for that," Recker said. "That's all her."

Vincent coughed, then cleared his throat. "Getting pleasantries out of the way, I'm sure you've got other things to do, so I'll get straight to the point on this one. I'm sure you're curious what this is about."

"Crossed my mind."

"The Scorpions. I'm hearing they have regrouped."

"Figured they would. I didn't expect them to take that beating and lick their tails and run. I assumed they'd be back."

"And they are. Now."

"I haven't heard anything."

"I have," Vincent said. "They've got new leadership in place and it looks like they're ready to do some things."

"What kind of things?"

"First is, they're looking to put down some roots. They're staying for a while."

"Well, I guess I'll have a little something to say about that."

"They're planning to have something to say about that too."

"What do you mean?"

"They know it was you behind that whole hospital thing."

"How?"

"Who else would it be?"

"Couldn't take one for the team and say it was you?" Recker said with a laugh.

"Doesn't suit my purposes at the moment."

Recker shrugged, not really concerned if they knew it was him or not. "Doesn't really matter."

"Maybe not yet. But let me tell you, my friend, they are gunning for you. You, right now, are their number one target. Their number one enemy. You. And you alone. And they are planning on zeroing in."

"That makes two of us. They're my number one target too. And I'm gonna zero in on them. And I am not gonna rest until the rest of them are put in the ground with their friends."

"I knew that would be your intention. I just wanted to warn you that they're planning on doing everything within their means to find you."

"Let them. I'm not afraid of them. How do you fit into this?"

"I don't. Not yet, at least. They're still planning on sidestepping me as much as possible for the moment. I don't see that changing until they get you out of the picture."

Recker smiled. "You mean if, don't you?"

"Of course. I've learned to never bet against you over the years, no matter what the odds."

"What about the leadership group? You know who it is?"

"Kind of similar to before. I believe they're using a three-headed monster so to speak. A three-man leadership group to make decisions for the bunch."

"Got names?"

Vincent reached into his pocket and removed a slip of paper, then slid it across the table. Recker picked it up and saw three names on it.

"Mind reading now?"

Vincent grinned. "I think I know you well enough by now to anticipate some of your questions."

"Know anything about these guys?"

"I've done some background on them, as I'm sure you will as well. Nothing that particularly stands out other than they're long-term members of the group. I think all exceeding ten years."

"So no new ideas or fresh concepts, probably. They'll stick to what they know best."

"Most likely."

"They can target me all they want, they're not gonna find me, so that's of no consequence to me."

"All it takes is one slip-up."

Recker shook his head. "Won't happen. Besides me, any ideas on what they got tabs on?"

"That I do not. With a group like that it could be almost anything."

"How do you know they're still planning on staying out of your way?"

"I had a meeting with these men yesterday," Vincent answered. "They assured me of such."

They talked for another twenty minutes or so, almost all of it about The Scorpions. By the time Recker left, he didn't feel any differently than he had before, but at least he had the names of the leaders now. They already had their names and faces from the check they did before, but now they knew who was calling the shots. When Recker exited the diner, Malloy escorted him outside. Along with the usual guard at the door, the three men made some small talk before Recker had to go. Recker happened to look across the street and saw a light blue car parked along the street, with a couple of men inside. As soon as Recker made eye contact, the men looked away. Recker didn't stare long, but looked long enough to recognize the two faces as Scorpion members. He continued talking to the other two men, not wanting to make a big deal out of it.

"Just so you know, you might wanna tell Vincent to change his eating habits," Recker said.

"Why?" Malloy asked.

"Don't look, just trust what I say."

"OK?"

"There's two Scorpions sitting across the street looking at us."

Malloy and the guard continued talking to Recker like he had never informed them of the men, giving the Scorpions no indication that they had been discovered.

"You sure?" Malloy asked.

"Positive. Recognize them from the pictures we got laid out in the office. It's them."

"I guess the question is now... what are they doing here? They looking to get tabs on Vincent's where-abouts and movements? Or are they looking for you?"

"Could be both," Recker replied. "They might be trying to find me first, then after I'm gone, then come after him. I think right now I'm their first priority."

"Makes sense."

"Either way, they're gonna have to be dealt with."

"You know anything about this meeting they had with Vincent yesterday?"

Malloy shook his head. "No, I didn't hear the details."

"Strange. Don't you always?"

Malloy grinned. "Not this time."

"Well, whatever the case, if they take off after I leave, you can be sure they're after me at the moment. If not, then it's you."

"I'll walk you to your car."

Recker thought it was an odd statement, considering Malloy had never offered to do that before. He knew something was up. Malloy wanted to talk to Recker in private, without the other guard listening in. He didn't want anyone to know he was talking about Vincent's business without authorization. That was a no-no in Vincent's world. And Malloy was in such good standing, he wasn't going to do it in front of other employees. As they walked to Recker's car, Malloy finally opened up.

"About this meeting yesterday, I did hear a few things."

"So you were there?"

"Possibly. Didn't want to say with wandering ears around."

They stopped and faced each other once they got back to Recker's SUV. "What do you know?"

"I know they're planning on putting a terror-lock-down on this city in the coming weeks. Bank jobs, violent robberies, assaults, you name it, they're planning on doing it. They want to put a fear into this city over what went down at the hospital. They especially want to send a message to you that you haven't won. They're angry. They know you were the one behind that."

"I figured they would assume it."

"They don't know the real reason behind it. You know, Mia and all. They think it was just about them. As far as I know, they don't know the connection between you. I just thought I'd let you know so you weren't wondering."

"I appreciate that."

"The other thing is they assume you have two partners, based on the hospital thing."

"I do."

"Yeah, but not the two that they think. They assume it's like a three-man squad that goes out there. So it's just you and Chris, but they think it's three of you out there instead of two."

Recker glanced over at the car across the street, not turning his head directly at them so they didn't think he noticed them. They were still there.

"You know anything about what they're planning?" Recker asked. "Any specifics?"

"No, just in general terms. I know they're planning on sending you a message somehow. How they're doing that, I don't know. But they said it's gonna be big and loud, so whatever that means."

"Thanks for the tips."

"Figured you should know."

"Wonder why Vincent didn't say."

"You know how it is. He won't say anything unless he thinks it's necessary. He likes being the one with the most knowledge and holding it over your head."

"So why are you telling me?"

Malloy looked past Recker and focused on a couple of other cars as he formulated the answer in his mind.

"I dunno. I guess because I think he's making a mistake with all this."

"How so?"

"He's letting The Scorpions play in his sandbox for a while instead of taking them out right away. You can't let guys like this get a foothold, because once they do, they'll want more, and more, and more. This thing they have with you is only a stepping stone for them. Once they feel you're out of the way, or they just go around you completely, it's only a matter of time before they go after him."

"So why's he hesitating on them so much?"

Malloy shook his head. "To be honest, I'm not sure. I thought it was just because he didn't want another war so close on the heels of Nowak, but I don't think that's it. We've got enough men to fight them."

"I thought so too."

"He hasn't said this, and I could be off base, but I think he's hoping that you take them out for him. If he lets you do it, he probably only has to give minimal support, he stays in the clear, he doesn't have to risk losing men, and you do all the heavy lifting for him."

"I kind of figured it was something like that."

"Like I said, though, that's just my gut feeling on it. He hasn't said that directly."

"It would make sense though."

"Yeah, well, if you need my help, you got it. Just ask."

"Vincent wouldn't like that."

Malloy sighed. "I know. But the person who's on top doesn't always see the big picture as clearly as the ones who are on the front line, do they?"

"I would agree with that."

"These guys are bad dudes and they need to be eliminated. I know a lot of people would think that's strange coming from someone like me."

"I don't."

"You're an exception. I've done a lot of bad things in my time, and some I should be locked up for, but I've never hurt someone who didn't deserve it or who didn't know what they were getting into. These guys hurt people just to hurt them. That's the difference."

Recker nodded, understanding what he was saying completely. "You hear anything about them recruiting?"

"Yeah, I think they got some feelers out there. Don't think it's in full swing yet though."

"Why not?"

"They need time to get people in and trust them. They've never had to do something like this before. You put a hurting on them. They've always just brought one or two people in every few months or so, you know, as things came along. They never had to go out and actively solicit people. They just came to them naturally. This is new territory for them. They gotta take their time to get the right people so they know who they're getting."

"That makes it better for us," Recker said. "But it

means we gotta hit them before they really do get more people in."

"I agree. Right now, there's what, fifty, sixty people? If we let them go for a while and they get in full recruiting mode, they could pick up another fifty, seventy-five guys. They gotta be taken out in full in the next couple of weeks."

"Take two or three out a day, piece of cake, right? Have it sewed up in three weeks."

Malloy smiled. "I was hoping for bigger chunks at a time. Why settle for smaller numbers?"

"So how you gonna swing working this without Vincent finding out?"

"I'll just tell him things come up that I gotta take care of. Won't be anything new or unusual. I'll just head out like I always do. Tell him the details later."

"Well when Scorpions start showing up dead the day after you're always ducking out, don't you think he's gonna put two and two together?"

"Not if I do it right."

"OK. I guess if something comes up that I need a hand with, I'll give you a call."

Malloy nodded. "And if I hear specifics on anything, I'll pass it along to you."

Recker then shook hands with him. "Sounds like a deal."

"What are you gonna do about them?" Malloy asked, barely giving a nod of his head, though it was clear he was referring to the Scorpions that were watching them.

"Oh. Guess I'm gonna have to duck them somewhere."

"Need a hand?"

"Why, got some free time?"

"Well, you wanna start taking them out? No time like the present. If they're after you, won't come back to Vincent at all. They'll assume it's your work."

"What'd you have in mind?"

"You keep driving to a specific place. I'll get a sniper in place. When they get there, we take them out."

Recker smiled. "You got a sniper on speed dial?"

"There's one here every time Vincent's here. Just in case."

Recker briefly looked at a few of the surrounding buildings, trying to figure out where the man would be located, though he couldn't initially see anything. It didn't surprise him though. A man like Vincent would always take the utmost precautions, especially after shots had been taken at him before.

"Vincent won't realize you're shifting your man around?"

Malloy shook his head. "Nah. I take care of all that. If you leave now, drive for about twenty minutes, stop, he'll take the shots, then be back before Vincent leaves."

"All neat and tidy."

"That's the idea. Vincent's usually got another hour here, so we gotta move quick if you wanna do it."

"Your man won't tell Vincent he was redirected?"

"He'll think the order came from him. It'll be fine, trust me. I know how to rework things. Don't worry about me."

"OK," Recker said, hopping into his car. "You're in the driver's seat."

3

As Recker pulled out of the parking lot, Malloy went back over to the front entrance of the diner. He stood there and made small talk with the guard, looking out of the corner of his eye at the car across the street. Once Recker got on the street and started driving away, the car with the Scorpions started up and drove after him. That was Malloy's cue. He got on his phone and called the sniper that was nearby.

"Hey, you see that blue car that just pulled out?" Malloy asked.

"Going the same direction as Recker?"

"That's it."

"Yeah."

"Two occupants. Front seat. Take them out."

"Where?"

"I'm gonna have Recker go to the warehouse down by the river. You know the one."

"When?"

"Get there now. The guys in the car are Scorpions."

"What about Recker?"

"He's fine. Pass."

"On my way."

"Let me know when it's done."

"Will do."

Recker drove for about ten minutes, not knowing exactly where he was going. He figured Malloy would call at some point. If he wanted to, he could have lost the Scorpions on his own. It wouldn't have been much of a challenge for him. But, Malloy was right. This way was better. They had to start eliminating Scorpions a little at a time, whenever they could find them. Once they started building their ranks again, the job would get infinitely tougher. As he was sitting at a light, with the car the Scorpions were in three cars behind him, Recker's phone finally rang.

"Down by the river," Malloy said. "Remember that little warehouse that we used to set Nowak up in?"

"I remember."

"Go in there and wait."

"Should I get out of my car?"

"Doesn't matter. My guy's on his way there. He'll be in place by the time you get there. That's why I waited to call you, so he could get there first."

"OK. I'm on my way there."

Recker made sure he didn't lose his tail, which was somewhat different for him. Usually, he was driving faster and with a lot more turns, weaving in and out of traffic. This time, he drove at a nice and steady pace, making sure the people behind him kept up with him. A couple of times, his normal instincts took over, and he had to consciously slow down, reminding himself that he wasn't trying to lose anybody on this occasion.

Recker arrived at the abandoned trucking facility after another twenty minutes in the car. The gate was slightly open, so Recker got out of his car to open it further. He got back in his car and drove all the way in, stopping once he got to the office building. He kept the gate open so his followers could come in as well, though he didn't know the exact plan on taking them out. That was the only part that really bothered him. He didn't know exactly how Malloy planned on taking them out, other than a sniper was probably already in place somewhere. Recker didn't like being kept in the dark about anything, especially when his life was involved. He got back out of the car again and milled around the front door. He kept peeking at the gate, waiting to see if the blue car had arrived yet, though he didn't see it. The door to the office was unlocked, so Recker went in. It didn't look like anything had changed since the last time he was there. It was still dusty, dirty, and unused.

Recker looked out the window, though he still didn't see the car. It wasn't waiting by the gate and it hadn't pulled in. While he was waiting, he called Jones to let him know where he was, since he didn't go right back to the office after the meeting.

"How's things there?" Recker asked.

"Fine. Is your meeting over?"

"Yeah. I, uh, took a detour on the way back."

"I'm sure you will explain that further, right?"

"When I came out of the diner, I noticed two Scorpions sitting across the street in a car. I assume they were looking for me, waiting for me to come out so they could tail me."

"How would they know you were there?"

"I don't know."

"I mean, that's kind of random, don't you think?"

"Could be they are following Vincent, hoping he would eventually meet me," Recker replied. "Might've had people set up all around the city hoping I'd show up."

"Possibly."

"Apparently, according to Vincent, I'm there number one target right now."

"Well that's hardly surprising."

"No, it's not. Vincent said he just had a meeting with their new leadership group yesterday. He gave me their names."

"Good."

"He also said they're planning on some big stuff. They're gonna be more violent than ever."

"Again, not that surprising."

"They also are planning on sending me some kind of message, though I don't know what that might be."

"Hmm. Sounds rather ominous."

"Yeah, and a little scary too," Recker said. "I just hope their message to me doesn't cost innocent people their lives."

"So I take it this detour of yours is trying to lose them following you?"

"Well, in a way, yeah, kind of."

"Would you like to explain that better?"

"I'm losing them permanently."

"Oh," Jones replied, knowing exactly what that meant. "How are you doing that? Or shouldn't I ask?" Jones knew it was sometimes better for his mental state if he didn't know all the details.

"I'm sure it'll please you to know that I'm not lifting a finger."

Jones hesitated before answering, not having a clue as to what was going on. "Uh, you did say you were losing them permanently, did you not?"

"Malloy is helping to diffuse the situation. I led the car here to the river, you know, where we did that thing with Nowak. He's got a sniper here who's gonna take them out."

"So Vincent is helping?"

"No, not quite. Malloy's doing this off the books."

"Wait a minute. You're telling me Malloy is authorizing killing Scorpions without his boss' approval."

"That's right."

"Uh, wow. That's kind of a powder keg in the making, don't you think?"

"Maybe," Recker answered. "Malloy seems to think it's not a problem so long as it's kept hush-hush."

"I don't know about that."

"Well, it's not really our problem."

"Why is Malloy interjecting himself into this situation?"

"He doesn't share Vincent's strategy, which I kind of question myself. Maybe he's got something bigger in mind, but I don't know why Vincent's taking a back seat on this. Anyway, Malloy knows the longer the Scorpions are allowed to remain here, the more Vincent's going to eventually become their target. Malloy knows it's better to get rid of them now than allow them to stay here for six months and build their troops back up. Now's the time to strike and get them out."

"As much as it pains me to say it, I agree. With every battle or conflict in history, the best time to strike was when the enemy was already reeling, before they had a chance to regroup. In theory, that time is now."

As they were talking, two loud booms rang out in the clear blue sky. Recker instantly looked through the window, knowing what that meant. Jones heard the pops as well.

"Oops. Looks like I gotta go."

"Should I ask?" Jones said.

"No, you shouldn't. I'll see you later."

Recker sprinted out of the office and got back in his car. He raced to the front gate, then got out of his car and looked down the street. He instantly saw the blue car parked across the street, only fifteen or twenty feet down. Recker got back in his car and slowly drove past the Scorpions, looking inside their vehicle as he passed. He saw both men in the front seats slumped over. The driver's head was resting up against the steering wheel, while the passenger was tilted on his side, his arm slightly hanging out the window. Recker knew it was pointless to look around to see where the shots came from, though he had a good general direction. He then looked in his rearview mirror and saw a tan car peel onto the street and race in the opposite direction. He thought about calling Malloy to let him know it was done, but he figured the sniper would do that, anyway.

There was nothing left for him to do now. Nothing but wait. Wait for the message that he knew was coming. And after the Scorpions found out what just happened with the crew that was following him, Recker was sure that message would come through a little louder, and a little clearer. He just hoped it was only meant for him and nobody innocent got caught up in it. Now, it was just a matter of when that message would be received.

4

R ecker was pinned down behind a bunch of crates, but was able to keep firing to ward off his attackers. He looked around to see how he was going to escape this one, though there didn't appear to be an easy answer. The door was clear on the other side of the room and there were no windows nearby. He counted at least six or seven Scorpions that he was up against. They traded shots back and forth for the next few minutes. There didn't seem like there was going to be an end to it. The Scorpions knew they had Recker pinned down. They didn't need to advance. He was eventually going to run out of ammunition, making killing him a much easier proposition for them.

After about five minutes of firing back and forth, Recker was down to his last few remaining bullets. He'd have to make them count. He stood up and hit one of the Scorpions, dropping him to the ground. Recker then felt a little woozy. His head started spinning. He suddenly felt cold. He looked down at his shirt and saw a small little hole in it. Red started pouring out of the hole, dripping onto the ground. He then looked back at his opponents and felt a rush of energy again. If this was going to be it, he was going to go down in a blaze of glory. He fired his last shots, hitting a couple more of them. He squeezed the trigger on his gun, but there were no more bullets left to fire. Recker looked at his adversaries and huffed, then tossed his gun on the ground. He stretched his arms out wide, waiting for the inevitable.

Just as Recker closed his eyes, he heard more gunfire. He didn't feel anything though. He opened his eyes and saw Haley burst through the door, eliminating the last of the Scorpions there. Once the last member dropped, Haley came over to his partner to check on him.

"You all right?"

"Yeah, I'll make it," Recker replied. "Let's just get out of here."

"I got the car just outside."

"You go ahead, get it started. I'll be out."

Haley left the room and went outside to start the car up. He was sitting in the driver's seat, waiting for his friend. Recker, walking a little slower, came out a minute later. He stopped by the door of the building and looked down at his injury, thinking it looked pretty bad. He then looked back at Haley, sitting in the car. Recker took a step towards the car, then was thrust back into the wall, thrown off his feet as the car exploded in front of him. Recker was groggy, moving his head around, as he lay face first on the ground. He looked *up and saw that the car his friend had been in was on fire, smoke rising into the air.*

"Chris! Chris!"

Recker got to his feet and stumbled his way to the car, putting his hand in front of his face to protect it from the extreme heat he was feeling. He looked at what remained of the car, which was torn apart from the explosion, and couldn't see his friend anywhere. He wiped a tear from the corner of his eye, realizing Haley was gone.

"That's supposed to be me. That's supposed to be me."

Recker woke up, feeling his arm shaking. He quickly jumped up, sitting up on the couch, seeing Mia tugging at his arm. He had a blank stare on his face. Mia hated looking at his eyes like that. It was like he wasn't really there. It was the case more often than not when he woke up from one of his dreams like that. It was a scary look.

"Where am I?" Recker said, still not totally with it yet.

"You're home." Mia rubbed his arm, then his shoulder, then sat down next to him and held him closer. "You're home." Mia's eyes started welling up with tears, hating to see him acting like this. She quickly was able to get herself back under control and wiped her tears away with her free hand.

"What am I doing here?"

"It's still morning. You woke up in the middle of the night, then went out to the kitchen for a drink. I guess you sat down on the couch and fell back asleep again."

"Oh. I don't remember. Did I, um... did I have another one?"

"I think you had two. When you woke up earlier, you looked startled, and then another one just now."

"What time is it?"

"Just after eight."

"I probably should get to the office soon."

"Just relax. The office can wait a little bit. Just get yourself together first."

Recker's mouth felt dry, and he tilted his head back to look up at the ceiling. He took a deep breath, his body feeling heavy, like something was anchoring him down. Mia continued to rub him, hoping to ease his tension and relax him, though it wasn't an easy chore. She could feel him laboring to breathe. She thought about mentioning him seeking help again, though she wasn't sure if this was the right moment. She wanted to at least wait until he seemed back to normal. There was no time frame for that either. It seemed as if with each passing nightmare that Recker had, the time that he needed to recover from it was taking longer and longer.

Instead of moving, Mia just leaned Recker back and held him in her arms for another twenty minutes. As the time went by, Recker's body slowly went back to normal. The tension eased up, his mind seemed more clear, and the haziness that clouded his senses went away. He didn't know what he would do without her. He was sure that he would probably be dead by now if

Mia wasn't in his life. She just had a way of healing him, making him feel better, just by her holding him and feeling her touch. Once he was back to feeling himself again, Recker looked over at his beautiful girl-friend and hugged her.

"I don't know what I would do without you."

Mia smiled. "I wonder about that myself."

They kissed, and hugged, and kissed some more for the next few minutes. Recker was really grateful to have her in his life. He knew he didn't deserve her. As they finally untangled from each other, they sat on the couch another couple of minutes. Mia figured now was the time to ask the question that she knew her boyfriend didn't want to talk about. Or hear. But she had to say it, anyway. She loved him too much not to.

"Mike, when are you gonna get help?"

"For what?" Recker asked, pretending he didn't know what she was talking about.

"For this. You gotta talk to someone."

"I am. I'm talking to you."

"But I'm not helping."

"You are. You help more than you know. Just be being here, by being you, you're what helps me get out of it."

"But that's not enough," Mia said, feeling her eyes get a little wet again. "You can't keep living like this. They're getting worse all the time. You know it."

"They'll eventually go away."

"But they're not. You've been having them for

months. They're not going away. They're getting worse. Before, you were getting them once in a while. Then every couple of weeks, then every week, now you're getting them three or four times every week, and sometimes several in the same night."

"It's just a phase, I'm sure. It'll get better."

"Why won't you please just talk to someone?"

"Because I can't."

"Mike, psychiatrists and therapists, they're not just going to run to the police and say, 'hey, I've got The Silencer over here, lock him up'. They're not going to do that. They will try and help you. But you've got to let them."

"You know me, trusting people I don't know is not an easy thing for me."

"I know. I know. I just... I just don't know how else we can get past this. How you can get past this. It's hurting you. And it's hurting me watching you deal with it. There just has to be another way."

Recker sighed and stared at the wall in front of him. He wasn't trying to be difficult. He knew how much this meant to Mia. And he knew him talking to someone was probably the right thing to do. But he didn't think he could just go to anybody. It had to be the right person. If he could find such a person, he would do it. Or, at least heavily think about it. He still wasn't sure if he could actually make his legs walk into a psychiatrist's office, but, at least the thought was there.

"I don't ask a lot of you," Mia said. "You know I don't. I put up with a lot, I don't nag you, I don't hound you to do things or not do things, but I'm really asking you to consider doing this. If not for you, then for me. Please?"

Recker looked at her, seeing the tears in her eyes, then planted a soft kiss on her lips. How could he look at her and refuse? He then wiped the tears from her eyes and nodded.

"I'll start looking into it."

Mia smiled. "You will? Are you just telling me that?"

"No, I mean it. I really will start looking into it. It's gotta be the right person though. That might take me some time, but I promise, if I find that person, then I'll go."

Mia sniffled and wiped her nose, then gave her boyfriend a hug. "Thank you. That will make me so happy."

"I might need your help in actually getting there, but, I'll give it a shot."

"You know I'll always be with you. Whatever you need. Always."

"I know."

They snuggled on the couch together until nine and then Recker reluctantly had to pull himself away, as much as he hated to. There was still a Scorpion problem that he had to attend to. Mia had to get herself ready for work soon anyway, so the two of them got dressed and ready at the same time. They both wound up leaving right around the same time and left together. Before parting in the parking lot to go to their separate cars, they kissed each other goodbye.

"Be safe out there."

Recker smiled. "As always."

"Uh, huh."

Recker got into his car and turned it on. Before he was able to put it in drive, his phone rang. It was Jones.

"I know, I know, I'm a little late. I'm coming. I'm on my way now."

"It's not that," Jones said.

"Oh. Got a job lined up?"

"Not exactly."

"Then what are you calling for?"

"You were wondering about that message from the Scorpions. It's been received. Loud and clear."

5

R ecker quickly got back to the office, finding Jones and Haley already at their desks. Jones never told him exactly what the message was, saying it was better if he saw it for himself.

"So what is this message?" Recker asked.

Jones moved his chair over so his partner could get a better look. He started playing a video on his computer. Recker leaned in closer to see better. The video was dark at first, but they could tell it was outside somewhere, though they couldn't tell the location. There were no words said, but there was some ominous, creepy music playing. After a few seconds, people appeared on the screen, and it was obvious they were at a cemetery. There were a bunch of men there, at least eight or ten, but none of their faces could be made out. They all either had hoods on, or masks, or bandanas covering their faces, and a few had all three.

"This is all very interesting," Recker said, not really impressed. "But..."

"It gets better," Jones said.

Recker continued watching as the men walked toward a bunch of graves. They eventually stopped near one. The video was a little shaky at first until the men stopped at one of the graves. The camera zoomed in on the headstone, revealing writing carved out in it.

The Silencer lies here. Killed by Scorpions. May he rot in Hell.

They then heard a lot of maniacal laughing as the video slowly faded to black. Then additional text came on the screen, in all caps and in white lettering.

STAY TUNED TO THE TV FOR PART 2!

"That it?" Recker asked.

"Isn't that enough?" Jones replied.

Recker shrugged. "Eh. I expected something more."

"Wait for part two," Haley said.

"Yeah, I wonder what that's about."

"I have a feeling we will find out shortly," Jones said.

"Whatever it is, it must be something that will get a lot of news coverage," Recker said. "They feel pretty confident it will be on TV. Only reason for that is if it really is something big."

"Are you not going to say something about what we just saw?"

"Bad camera work."

Jones rolled his eyes. "I'm talking about the content."

"Oh yeah, how'd you get it?"

"It was sent to Vincent since he's in contact with both parties. They figured he would pass it along, so he did."

"Oh."

"That's not the issue. They already have a grave picked out for you, Michael."

"So?"

"So? Does that not bother you in the slightest?"

"Not really," Recker answered. "David, people have been trying to kill me since I was twenty years old. You get used to death threats after a while."

"I'm kind of hurt," Haley said. "They didn't mark a grave for me."

Recker laughed. "Maybe they didn't know what to call you. Maybe we should come up with a nickname for you too, that way you can have your own fan club."

Haley nodded, looking like he was actually thinking about it.

"I can't believe you two," Jones said. "Here we are getting death threats from a dangerous group and you two are making jokes."

"It's really not that big of a deal," Recker said.

"I wonder where that grave is," Haley said.

"Yeah, can you figure out where that is?"

"Why, are you planning to visit?" Jones asked.

"Just curious."

"I might be able to, though I don't see of what importance knowing the location is."

"Well, I assume they picked a location that's either familiar to them or close. Could give us a hint about where they are now."

"Hmm, that's true. I'll start running the video and overlapping it with all the cemeteries in the area."

"Good. Maybe we'll get something out of it."

"So seeing your name on a grave doesn't do anything for you?"

Recker put his hand on his stomach. "Makes me a little hungry. I skipped breakfast."

"Doesn't worry you at all, huh?"

"Not a bit. I'm more worried about what part two is gonna be. I can handle myself. This is what I signed up for. Other people aren't so lucky."

"Maybe Vincent can tell us something about how he got the video," Haley said. "Who it was, where he got it, that kind of stuff."

"I've already enquired," Jones said. "It's a dead end. Vincent was contacted, asked if he could deliver something to The Silencer, a package, and he agreed. Malloy was dispatched to pick up the package at a set location. He took it, then contacted me about it."

"You?" Recker asked. "Why you? Wonder why he didn't call me first?"

"He did apparently. He said he tried to call you and got no answer, so then he turned to me."

Recker hadn't even looked at his phone yet, other than taking the call from Jones when he left his apartment. He then pulled his phone out, then looked at his call history. There was Malloy's name, calling him at seven-fifteen and again at seven-thirty. He didn't leave a voicemail though.

"Huh. I guess he did try calling me."

"Yes, well, anyway," Jones said, continuing. "He called me and asked about meeting me somewhere to deliver it. I just told him to open it if he felt safe about it. You know, in case it was a bomb or something. So he did, told me it was some kind of flash drive. I let him watch it first, then he emailed it to me. So that's the long version of how I acquired it."

"Oh. As long as it was short and easy."

"You're not taking this threat seriously at all, are you?"

"Oh, I take the Scorpions very seriously," Recker replied. "I know they're bad guys, they mean business, absolutely. But this video, nah, I don't take that seriously. That's just theatrics. That's just them being cute. That doesn't bother me. Seeing my name on a grave, that's just them being funny. What worries me more is what this part two's gonna be. That's what worries me."

"I wonder how long they're gonna make us wait for that?" Haley asked. "Wonder if it'll be soon or if it'll be an all day thing."

"You haven't picked up anything with your software have you?"

"Nothing that I can definitely trace back to them," Jones answered. "There are a few things in the works, but nothing that traces back to any of their known members. I have already checked those leads out."

"So whatever it is, they're keeping it hush-hush."

"Or they're just only meeting in person to discuss it," Haley said.

"Maybe if we try to think about what kinds of things they could make an impact with that would make it onto TV we can come up with something," Jones said.

"That could be just about anything," Recker said. "Murder, kidnapping, blowing something up, robbing a bank, any of those and probably a hundred other things that could qualify."

"I hate just sitting here with no leads, waiting for the other shoe to drop," Haley said.

"I know. I don't think we have any other choice though. Not without something to go on."

"We could go out and start cruising, see if we stumble on anything."

"You know what the odds of us finding that something are?"

"Hundred million to one?"

"At least. I think that's all we can do right now. Wait."

The three of them continued working on the computers, trying to find something, hoping their software program would alert them to something. But it was a fruitless effort. Recker called Tyrell and got him involved, hoping he could find something out on the street level. They worked straight through most of the day, hardly taking any breaks at all, in hopes of finding out what the Scorpions were planning. It didn't matter though. They still came up empty. Recker leaned back in his chair and let out a loud, audible sigh in frustration, while Haley tossed a pencil down on the desk, and Jones got up to start walking around and stretch his legs. He put the TV on while he was up. It was four-thirty and the local news was just about to start. Maybe whatever was supposed to happen already happened. It didn't take long for them to figure out what part two was. It was the lead story. The team focused in on the broadcast as the news anchor started talking.

"Today, our lead story is a warehouse explosion that completely decimated the building you're about to see via footage from our helicopter," the woman said.

The screen then turned to the video feed from the helicopter, which was circling over the building. The fire from the building was just about put out now, but they also showed footage from earlier in the day, when the fire was burning much worse.

"The explosion happened roughly four hours ago at this warehouse building in West Philadelphia, which has apparently been closed down for about five months now since the previous tenants moved to a new location. Early reports indicate that there are thankfully no casualties, though police are still investi-

43

gating at the scene. There are also words spray painted around the building on the ground with the words Silencer. It's unclear if this is the work of the famed Silencer or someone sending him a message. For more, we go to our correspondent on the scene, Tom Jennings. Tom, you have more for us about this?"

"Yes, Clarissa, I'm actually standing here with Lieutenant Wilcox of the police department, what can you tell us about this so far?"

"Well at this point we're still investigating, but it appears the building was empty so there were no casualties, no victims, the fire is just about put out now, so we'll be going in shortly to determine the cause of the fire."

"Is arson or foul play suspected at this time?"

"I would say that's probably likely," Wilcox replied.

"Now the words Silencer are written prominently throughout the area, do you think the famed vigilante is responsible for this?"

"Uh, it's difficult to say. It certainly would seem unlikely at this point, as it goes completely against his usual M.O. to advertise his work. He's never done that before. But nothing can be completely ruled out at this time."

"So if it wasn't him, then somebody must be talking to him or making this an example for him, wouldn't you say?"

"That's certainly possible."

"Do you have any other suspects at this time?"

"Right at this moment, no, but we'll be combing through security footage throughout the area to see if we can pick someone up, as well as obtaining evidence from inside of the building, so it's still early."

"OK. That's it from here, Clarissa. The good news, no injuries. But it will probably be several days before we learn more about what happened here today. Back to you."

The screen turned back to the news anchor, who then started talking about a different topic. Jones instantly put the sound on mute, not interested in hearing about anything else at the moment. He turned to his partners to collect their thoughts on what they just witnessed.

"Well? Would anybody like to go first?"

"At least there was nobody in that building when it blew up," Haley said. "That's the good news."

"Yeah," Recker said. "I think that's what would be considered the warning shot. It's just to let us know what's coming and the damage they can inflict."

"Hopefully, the police will realize this wasn't our work," Jones said.

"It won't come back to us. They know I'd never put my signature on something like that."

"Probably. But you never know."

"I don't think we have to worry about that. What we do have to worry about is what their next move is."

"It's a cinch that whatever it is, there'll be bodies

behind it," Haley said. "This was just to let us know what they can do."

"I agree. The next time I don't think we'll be so lucky."

"So what do we do now?" Jones asked. "How do we stop them without knowing what their plans are?"

Recker leaned back in his chair and closed his eyes. He didn't have an answer. At least not a good one. It was one of those rare times when he wasn't sure what to do. Nothing struck him as being worthwhile. Then his phone rang. He assumed it was Vincent to talk about the news item they just saw. It wasn't though.

"Tyrell, what's up?"

"Hey, heard about what happened on the news."

"Yeah, just saw it myself."

"How'd you like to get a little payback?"

"Uh, that's always the plan," Recker said.

"Well, you might wanna come down here right now then. I got four Scorpions standing in front of me."

Recker immediately sat up straight, his eyes almost bulging out upon hearing the news. "You got what?"

"Yeah, you heard right. I got four, bonafide, regular, grade-A, dues-paying members of that clan, standing a few feet away from me."

"How'd you manage to pull that off?"

Tyrell pretended to sound insulted. "Man, how many times do I gotta tell you? I am just that good at my job."

"They just walked in where you happened to be, didn't they?"

"Why you always gotta be raining down on my parade?"

"How do you know it's them?"

Tyrell rolled his eyes. "How do I know it's them, he says. How do I know it's them? Because they match the pictures you gave me. It's them. Geez, man, you want these dudes or not?"

"Yeah, I want them. Just making sure it's them."

"It's them, it's them, I guarantee it's them. They also haven't minded telling everyone in this place about them being Scorpions. Trying to intimidate everyone and run roughshod over everybody."

"Where are you at?"

"This place in North Philly called Stewie's. You know it?"

"Uh, yeah, I think I passed by it a time or two. What are they doing right now?"

"Right now? Playing pool. They've also been drinking a little. Maybe by the time you get here they'll be plastered out of their mind and make it easy for you."

"That would be nice. Easier is better, right?"

"Usually."

"All right. We'll be down in a bit. Call me if anything changes or they leave or anything."

"You know it."

Recker tapped Haley on the shoulder. "C'mon, we gotta go."

Jones looked perplexed. "Would you mind explaining where it is that you are going?"

"Tyrell said there's four Scorpions in a place called Stewie's."

"And you are going to go there and meet them?"

"We are," Recker said, walking over to his cabinet.

As he and Haley took out their guns, Jones didn't seem so sure about their plans.

"Maybe we should think about this first?" Jones said.

"What's there to think about?" Recker replied. "They're after us, we're after them, we've located them in this place, seems pretty straightforward to me."

"Yes, but let's just think about it first and make sure it's the right move. It's kind of suspicious that they're suddenly known in this place, immediately after what we just saw on the TV, is it not?"

"What, you think they're trying to set us up? How would they even know it'd get back to us that we'd know?"

"Tyrell is there?"

"Yeah."

Jones raised an eyebrow. "Unless they know he works with us. Nowak knew."

It gave Recker something else to think about, though he wasn't sure he was ready to go all in with that line of thinking yet. But it was certainly something he had to keep in the back of his mind.

"I think we still gotta go," Haley said. "If they don't know, this is another good chance to weaken their numbers."

"I agree," Recker said.

"And if they're waiting for you?" Jones asked.

"We'll be careful."

Jones knew they were going, so there was no point in debating the topic further. Recker watched him, though, as he went back to his chair and sat down.

"Is something else bothering you?"

Jones looked at him for a second, not sure he wanted to answer. But he eventually did. "It's just... we started this with the intention of helping people. I hate it when we go out with the explicit intention of killing."

"Hey, if you know of another way to get rid of these guys then I'm all for it."

Jones shook his head. He knew there was no other way. It didn't mean he liked it though. Recker didn't have the same objections, not that he enjoyed killing, but he didn't have reservations when he knew it was the only way.

"If you wanna look at it another way, you saw what they did to that warehouse. You know what they did at that hospital."

"Yes."

"You know there's more of that coming if we don't stop them now. And the bodies will pile up."

"I know."

"Sometimes, in order to prevent others from suffering a gruesome fate, you have to be proactive to make sure that doesn't happen."

Jones nodded, agreeing with everything that was said. He knew Recker was correct in his outlook. The Scorpions were a mean, nasty bunch, that did not hold the welfare of others very high. If they remained, a significant amount of people, good people, would probably be killed as a byproduct of their exploits. The only way to get rid of them was to eradicate them from existence.

Once Recker and Haley finished getting ready, they walked over to the door, ready to leave. Haley walked out, but Recker stopped and looked back at Jones, who was just staring at his computer.

"David."

Jones looked back. "Yes?"

"We got this. Don't worry."

6

As they drove to Stewie's, Recker texted Tyrell every few minutes to make sure the Scorpions were still there. They were. By the time Recker and Haley got there, they scouted the area out first, making sure there were no friends waiting nearby. If they saw a familiar face standing along the street, or a group of men in a car, or a bunch of people standing alongside the building, a face sticking out a window across the street, then they would know they had more to worry about. They saw none of that though. They continued cruising around for an extra few minutes, just to make sure. Once they were positive, they got out of their car and started walking around.

Recker and Haley walked around to the back of the building to pick out a good spot. It was a small alley behind a group of buildings. The only thing back there was mostly green dumpsters, and maybe a few chairs by the doors for workers who wanted to sit while they were on break.

"How you wanna work this?" Tyrell texted.

"Can you get those guys behind the building?" Recker replied.

"How am I gonna do that?"

"You're good at talking and improvising."

"Yeah, thanks."

"Can you do it?"

"Yeah, I'll figure out a way. You'll have to be ready because I can't guarantee I can give you notice."

"We're ready."

Recker and Haley were both stationed behind a different dumpster, not too far apart, but both along the far wall to make sure that they didn't catch each other in crossfire. As they were getting ready, Tyrell finished his drink by the table by the window, thinking about how he was going to get the four men outside. After a minute, he figured it out.Tyrell got out of his seat and walked over to the pool table, standing there for a few seconds watching the game. The Scorpions didn't really like people around them though, especially if they didn't have business with them.

"Something you want, dude?" one of them asked. "If not, you better shove off."

Another one walked over to Tyrell and gave him a little shove in the chest, making him stumble back a few steps.

"Uh, yes, I can see you fine gentlemen are busy here, but I had some information for you I thought you might be interested in."

"I doubt you got anything we'd be interested in," the man said.

"Umm, yeah, well, you guys are Scorpions, right? I mean, I heard you bragging about it earlier."

All four men stopped playing their game, stood up straight, and stared at him, wondering what he was up to. "You got something to say?"

Tyrell put his arms up, seeing that they were starting to get on edge. "Hey, man, it's all cool. Just wanted to talk a little business."

"We're not talking. Beat it before we lose our tempers."

"All right, all right, if you don't wanna know where The Silencer is, that's fine with me."

Tyrell turned around and started walking away before he was stopped. "Wait!"

Tyrell smiled and turned back around. "Yes?"

"You got information on The Silencer?"

"I do."

"So what is it?"

"Gentlemen, in all business deals, there's a give and take here. We both give something."

"What do you want?"

Tyrell smiled widely again. "Well, I figure information like this would be worth something substantial. Say, fifty-thousand?"

The men looked at each other. "We'll have to get back to you."

"This info is good for today only. Can't guarantee where The Silencer will be after this or if I will know. It's a now or never proposition."

"Give me a minute."

The lead Scorpion got on the phone and called his superiors, telling them about the situation. They were given the green light to go ahead with the plan.

"All right, looks like we're good," the man said. "What do you got?"

"Umm, the money?"

"We don't exactly carry around that kind of money on us you know. Don't worry, if the information is good, you'll get it."

"I guess I'll just have to trust you."

"So what do you have?"

Tyrell looked around the room. "Not here. Too many listening ears if you know what I mean. Can't have this coming back to me. Silencer's got snitches everywhere, man." Tyrell looked around the room once more, then pointed to the back door. "Let's go out there, all right? Should be safe."

The Scorpions agreed to talk outside, so Tyrell led them over to the back door. It wasn't locked or alarmed, as people periodically went out there throughout the day.

"I'll stay here," one of them said. "You guys fill me in."

Tyrell mumbled under his breath, making sure he wasn't heard, unhappy his plan was already crumbling. At least he was getting three of them to go with him. Once the shooting started, he was sure the fourth would soon follow, anyway. It would have just been nice to have them all together to start with. When Tyrell went outside, he immediately started looking around for his friends, hoping they didn't start blasting with him in the middle. Once the last Scorpion came out, he closed the door behind him. Tyrell kept looking around.

"What are you looking for?"

"Can't be too careful, man," Tyrell replied. "Just making sure everything's in the clear."

"It's clear, it's clear. What do you got?" Tyrell still kept looking, making the Scorpions nervous. "What do you keep looking for?"

"I'm not looking for anything. I'm listening."

"For what?"

Tyrell began to talk loudly, hoping that Recker, and Haley would hear him wherever they were. "I am listening for a sign. A sign!"

"A sign of what?"

"Probably us!" Recker said, jumping out from behind a dumpster. Haley did the same.

"It's you!" one of the Scorpions said, instantly reaching for his gun.

As all of the Scorpions started to reach for their weapons, Tyrell dove out of the way, trying to roll his way to safety. Recker and Haley already had their guns out, so mowing down the three men in front of them was not a problem. Two of the Scorpions actually were able to remove their guns, but they never got a chance to fire them. All three were dead in a matter of seconds.

Recker looked over at Tyrell, who was still on the ground. "Thought you said there were four of them?"

Tyrell pointed at the door, which just opened up again. The last of the Scorpions, hearing the shots from inside, rushed through the door with his gun already drawn. Recker immediately turned back to the door, though it wasn't necessary at that point. Haley had already taken care of the problem and shot him before the man had a chance to fire at anyone. The fourth member of the Scorpions fell on top of one of his buddies. Haley checked on the condition of the bodies as Recker went over to Tyrell and helped him up.

"You all right?"

"Man, could you have made that any closer?" Tyrell asked.

"Well I was waiting for you to get out of the way."

"Well I was waiting for you to let me know you were ready."

Recker smiled. "Already told you that."

Tyrell looked at him like he was thinking of something. "Oh yeah, you did, didn't you? Oh well."

Recker patted him on the shoulder. "It all worked out."

Haley came over to them a few seconds later. "They're all dead."

"Good. Let's get out of here before people start showing up."

They ran down the alley until they got to their car and hopped in.

"Guess I can't show my face there again," Tyrell said.

"Why not?" Recker asked.

"I go out the door with four men, who all wind up dead a few seconds later. Put two and two together, man."

"It'll be fine."

"People know you there?" Haley asked.

"I been there a time or two."

"Because when the police show up, will people there identify you?"

"Oh crap, I didn't even think about that. Great. Just great. Now if anybody says I was with them, the police will be knocking down my door."

"You'll be fine," Recker said.

"I'm glad you say so."

"Even if someone identifies you as talking to them, it's no big deal. You just say you were outside talking to them, they wanted you to find out about The Silencer. You agreed you would, then you left, then you don't know what happened after that."

"Yeah, I guess that might work."

"It'll work. You don't have a gun, didn't have one at

the time, and even if they tested you for residue, it'd come up clean. You got nothing to worry about."

"I love how you're so calm about everything."

"I'm so calm because there's nothing to worry about."

"Uh, huh."

"I better call David to let him know so he can keep his ears open to see if there's any blowback on this."

"And to see if there's any retaliation," Haley said.

"Yeah, that too."

"What do you want me to do now?" Tyrell asked.

"We'll drop you back off at your place in case the police come knocking. Just stay there the rest of the day. Don't need them putting an alert out on you or anything. Think you can handle that?"

"What? Please! Don't act like this is my first time waiting for the po-po to show up for something. I can handle them."

"Just stick to the story and you'll be fine."

"I got it."

Recker and Haley drove Tyrell back to his place and dropped him off, then headed back for the office. Once they got there, roughly an hour had passed since the shooting. Jones was at his desk typing away.

"Anything yet?" Recker asked.

"No, not a thing," Jones answered.

"They know about the bodies, right?"

"Uh, yes, that much is clear. The police are at the

scene. But in terms of anything after that, the outlook is not as clear."

Recker then looked at Haley. "Guess we wait."

"For what?" Haley replied.

"The other shoe to drop."

7

The team had been working feverishly over the past twenty-four hours, trying to get another line on the Scorpions. They knew the group wasn't going to just lie down, especially after four more of their group had been killed. For Recker and company, they just worried that another incident was going to happen and innocent people would get hurt or killed, before they were able to find the criminal gang again. Right now, Recker just wanted the Scorpions to be so focused on him, and trying to prevent his next attack, that they would forget any of the other stuff they were planning.

As they were working away, Recker's phone started ringing. He had left it on the counter by the fridge, and went over to pick it up. He wasn't necessarily surprised to see it was Tyrell, figuring he'd be hearing from him soon.

"Hey, I don't have to come bail you out right now, do I?"

Tyrell let out a laugh. "What? Don't be silly."

"Cops talked to you?"

"Yeah, they were here yesterday. Just like you said, no sweat."

"Stick to the story?"

"Yeah, they bought it, so I'm in the clear."

"Good. Got anything else for me?"

"Nah, I just wanted to let you know I'll be out and about today, seeing what I can dig up since I was grounded yesterday."

"All right, let me know if you find anything."

Recker hung up and started walking back to the desk when his phone rang again.

"Somebody is popular today," Jones said.

"It's a curse to be so cool and good-looking," Recker joked.

"Yes, but I've managed."

Everyone in the room smiled as Recker answered the phone. "Hey."

"Boss wants to know if you're available later," Malloy said.

"What for?"

"He's apparently trying to facilitate a meeting between you and the Scorpions."

"Why?"

"Beats me. Scorpions came to him and asked if they

could get in touch with you for a sit-down. What it's about, I don't know."

"What time?"

"About three hours."

"I'll be there."

"Same place as last time."

"Count me in."

Once Recker got off the phone, he stood there, thinking. Jones noticed him staring and knew what that usually meant.

"So what is the trouble?" Jones asked.

"Huh? No trouble."

"So where are you going?"

"What?"

"You said that you were going somewhere."

"Oh. That was Malloy. He said the Scorpions wanna meet at Vincent's."

"What?"

"That could be dicey," Haley said.

"And dangerous. There is no way we should agree to that," Jones said.

"Why not?" Recker asked.

"Because it's obviously some kind of setup. It's a trap."

"Could be."

"There is no could be about it," Jones said, standing firm. "There is no way this is legit. They are frustrated, angry, and don't know what else to do, and they can feel their ranks slipping away, so they will use this meeting as some kind of diversion to mask their real intentions."

"Probably."

"Probably? You agree that there is some ulterior motive and yet you still plan on going, anyway?"

"Yep."

"What is wrong with you?"

"Listen, we don't know where they are right now, right?" Recker asked. "After this meeting, if we do it like last time, we'll know where they are. At least a couple of them."

"Assuming they don't kill you first."

"David, you always think the worst."

"And you don't think enough about the worst."

"Listen, they're obviously going to try and use this meeting to do something. Probably after it's over. If Chris stays in the background, like last time, we can see what it is. I'm not going in blind. If we wanna try and eliminate this group as quickly as possible, this is one way to do that."

"And what if they're planning some type of all-out assault with thirty guys on you?" Jones asked.

"Then at least we'll know where most of them are."

Jones threw his hands up. "I know there is no debating with you on this. I know you're going to go do it, so anything I say is just going in one ear and out the other."

"No, it's not. I hear what you're saying, and I agree

63

that they're going to try something. I just think we can turn the tables on them."

"I would just rather wait until we're forcing the hand instead of reacting to whatever they do."

"Not always possible."

"I know that. But that would be my preference."

"Well that would be my preference too, but sometimes you just gotta play the cards you've been dealt." Jones nodded, knowing he was losing the argument. "You know, maybe it would be a good idea if you were out there too this time."

"What? Me? What good would I do with a gun? You know I'd probably be more of a hindrance than a help."

"No, I don't mean like that," Recker said. "You could still bring a tablet or something to work if you need to. I just mean having an extra pair of eyes on the street."

"That could work," Haley said. "Nobody knows you."

"Vincent does," Jones replied.

"Vincent and Malloy are going to be inside," Recker said. "Down the street from that warehouse is a bus stop. If you were to sit on the bench for a while, you could give a heads up if you saw anything."

"Such as?"

"Well, you know the faces of the Scorpions as well as we do. If you see them setting up across the street, or see one poking out a window, or one just cruising up and down the street. You should be able to see something, right?"

"I guess in theory."

"That should work," Haley said. "That would free me up to roam around and take anybody out that I see. And then if somebody tails Mike when he's leaving, I can follow, and David can see anything happening after we leave."

"Seems like a plan," Recker said. "What do you say?"

"I think we should all have our heads examined," Jones answered.

"Too late for that."

"Undoubtedly."

"So?"

"OK. Fine."

"Let's pull up a map of the area so we can start figuring things out," Recker said.

Jones pulled up an image of the area and printed it out so Recker could start marking things off on it. He showed Jones where he wanted him to set up. Haley was already familiar with the area and knew all the buildings around. They figured it was unlikely that anything would go down right then and there. They didn't appear to want to get Vincent riled up yet, and killing someone at his place would surely do that, so the team was fairly confident that whatever the Scorpions were planning, it would happen after the meeting was over.

They took the next hour to go over their plans and make sure they were a hundred percent on board and confident with it, especially Jones since he wasn't used to being in the field with them. Once they were good to go, they left, wanting to get on the scene in plenty of time. They figured the Scorpions would be doing the same, so if they got there ahead of them, they could see when the criminal gang got there. At least in theory. And if the Scorpions got there first, they should be able to have enough time to scout around and find them. Most of them anyway. Assuming that the Scorpions were planning what they suspected them of.

Once everyone was satisfied with the plan, the team left the office. Recker, Jones, and Haley all drove to the area in separate vehicles, that way nobody would be stranded if they all had to go in different directions. When they got to the area, they all put in their earpieces and made sure they weren't seen together, just in case Scorpions were already there. Jones parked along the street, just beyond where the bus stop was. He didn't want to be sitting there too long, having people wonder why he was at a bus stop and not getting on any buses after several of them had departed. That would be a dead giveaway if anyone noticed him sitting there for a long period of time. Recker and Haley drove around the area several times, on the lookout for any signs of potential trouble. At first they didn't notice anything. Then Haley radioed in.

"Hey, think I just saw something."

"What?" Recker asked.

"Tall building across from the warehouse. Saw a guy walking in with a suitcase."

"So?"

"His face looked familiar. Can't say for certain, but it could've been a Scorpion."

"And maybe he's bringing a rifle with him?"

"Could be."

"OK. I'll keep driving around for a little bit, you check that out."

"I'm on it."

As Haley drove into the parking lot of the building to check out their suspected sniper, Recker turned a corner, observing a car sitting there with a few occupants inside. He took a good look at them as he passed them by.

"Looks like we got one car with two or three inside," Recker reported. "David, see anything on your end?"

"Not yet. Looks pretty clear."

"Keep watching."

"That is what I'm here for, is it not?"

Recker resisted the urge for another sarcastic comment, and instead kept his eyes peeled as he roamed through the streets. He turned another corner and saw another car parked along the street. It also had a couple familiar looking faces sitting inside.

"Got another one."

"It appears as though they are making sure you don't slip away this time," Jones said.

"Who said I was planning on it? If they wanna fight. I'll fight."

"As long as it is strategically viable, Michael. No need to get all macho and get into a situation that's too big for your britches."

"David, nobody uses britches anymore. I'm pretty sure that went out with the Civil War."

"You get my meaning just the same." Before Recker was able to reply, Jones finally had some action on his front. "It looks like a car pulled up in front of me."

"Right in front of you?"

"Well not right in front. It's a little ways away. But it's in front. Just down a bit."

"Can you see inside?"

"Not really, but it's facing the entrance of the warehouse. I would think they might be watching to see who comes in and when."

"And let the others know when I leave," Recker said.

"That too."

"Chris, how you making out?"

"Checking out the rooms now," Haley answered. "The building is partially occupied, so I'm trying to get into the rooms that aren't. Just starting on the ground floor and going up."

"They'll probably be up top."

"Yeah, I figured as much. Just don't wanna take

anything for granted and miss something if they decide to be unorthodox."

"Let me know if you find something."

Recker continued driving around for a while until it got closer to the meeting time. He didn't see any other cars other than the three that were already noted.

"Mike, it's almost that time," Jones said.

"Yeah, I know. You see Vincent go in yet?"

"Looked like his car pulled in about five minutes ago."

"What about Scorpions?"

"No other cars have gone in beside Vincent's."

"Well let me know when they get there."

"Why?"

"I prefer to arrive last."

"For what purpose?"

"I like to make a grand entrance."

"Oh. Should I get the cape and crown out of the trunk for you? That should really spruce things up."

"Maybe it would at that," Recker said.

"Have you given thought as to how you are going to get away from all these cars out here?"

Before Recker had a chance to respond, Haley jumped in. "I have. Leave it all to me. By the time I'm finished, you should only have to worry about one car, and that's the one David's got his eyes on. I'll take care of the rest."

"You sure about that?" Recker asked.

"I've got it. Trust me."

"All right then. Looks like I can take the day off then."

"If all goes according to plan."

"How often does that happen?"

"Every once in a while. Let's hope today's one of those days."

8

Recker drove around for another ten minutes, being careful to not pass by the cars the Scorpions were in too often out of fear of getting spotted. But he wasn't going into Vincent's property before his visitors got there, just in case there was no meeting planned. It occurred to him that maybe they set up a phony meeting, just to get him in the area so they could try to pick him off. If that was the case, he wasn't going to make it easy for them. But that didn't seem to be the case. At least about the phony meeting part. Jones reported in a few minutes later.

"Michael, looks like our friends have now arrived."

"If they're friends, I'd like to know what you consider an enemy."

"Figure of speech," Jones said. "You know what I meant."

"OK. I'll give them another two or three minutes before I show up."

"Certainly are taking your time."

"There's a lot of moving parts here. I wanna make sure it all goes smoothly. Chris, how you making out?"

"Good. I've identified where the sniper is."

"Good. How much time you need?"

"Give me about ten minutes."

"I can do that."

"When you want me to start?" Haley asked.

"As soon as you're ready."

"Let the games commence then."

"Just update us on your progress as you go along."

"You got it."

Recker then drove to the front of the warehouse building, getting greeted by a couple of Vincent's men. They knew him well by this point and didn't need to get clearance to let him through. Vincent had already given them that order. As usual, Malloy was waiting for him by the front door. They shook hands before going inside.

"I think they're here for some kind of peace offering," Malloy said. "At least that's what I got out of it."

"Peace my ass. They've got a sniper in the building across the street, and three cars out on the street waiting for me."

"What?"

"Chris is out there. He thinks he can take care of the sniper and two of the cars."

"What about the third one?"

Recker shrugged. "Guess I'll have to do that one myself."

"Where these guys at?" Recker then gave him the street names that the cars were parked on. "I don't know if I can spare anybody at the moment. Everyone here is on Vincent's protection team. He'll ask questions if I take someone off their post and he isn't back in time or something happens."

"Don't worry about it. Chris said he can take care of it, so, he will."

Malloy nodded, though he still wished he could do more. "If not, I can make a call and get a couple guys here. Might take about fifteen minutes though."

"I think we're OK."

"All right. If you change your mind, just give me some type of signal."

As they were walking to the meeting room, Haley burst through the locked door in the building across the street. They were on the sixth floor of the eight story building. As soon as he crashed through it, the sniper rushed from his window to try to greet his surprise visitor. There were white sheets covering furniture, along with patches on the walls where holes used to be. It looked like it was getting ready to be painted. Whoever was working on it would have a new problem once they discovered a dead body in it. As soon as he crashed through the door, Haley rolled over, ignoring the pain from his shoulder from partaking in such an action. He quickly made his way behind what looked like a desk, judging by the shape it took underneath the white sheet, and waited for the sniper to charge in from the other room. It only took a few seconds.

The man didn't charge in like Haley had hoped, instead standing by the corner of the wall opening that led into the next room. Unfortunately for him, he picked the wrong side, as Haley still had a good line of sight on him. Haley aimed his gun and fired. The sniper immediately went down, though Haley didn't think he was gone yet. Haley quickly rushed around the desk and ran over to him before he had a chance to get back on his feet or regain his composure after being shot. Haley's instincts were right, as the man wasn't dead. But he was severely wounded. Just not enough to die yet. The man was still in the fight though and reached over for his rifle, which had been knocked out of his hand after the impact from the bullet. Haley ran in, saw the man reaching for his gun, and fired one more bullet. This time, there was no coming back from it. The man's arm went limp as the last remaining breath was exhaled from his system. With his first target down, Haley sped out of the room, ready to conquer his next victim.

"Sniper's down."

The words had just entered Recker's ear as he walked into the room. He saw Vincent sitting towards the end of the table to his left. Then the faces of two

Scorpions sat in the middle, staring straight at him. There was anger in their expressions, judging by their frowns and lack of emotion. Before sitting down, Recker shook hands with Vincent as Malloy closed the door. He then stared at his two opponents across the table before sitting down.

Recker looked at the men and grinned. "I'd shake your hands but I haven't got my tetanus shot yet."

The two Scorpions looked at each other and laughed. "Funny guy," Jed Naylor said.

"I do my best."

"I don't think comedy suits you best though. You should stick to what you're good at."

"I will. The next time I'll be laughing is at your funeral." Naylor didn't look like he enjoyed Recker's sense of humor. "What are we here for? Laughs? Or do you have something you wanna say?"

"Yeah, I got something I wanna say. How'd you enjoy that video? You seen it yet?"

"Are you referring to the one in the cemetery?"

"Yeah, that's the one."

Recker shrugged. "It was amusing I guess. Camera work wasn't great, acting was subpar, the lighting was horrendous, I mean, you're really not gonna win any awards for that type of stuff. You're really gonna have to step up your game."

"You really are a funny guy, aren't you?"

"Was that video supposed to scare me?" Recker asked. "Make me nervous? Shake in my boots? Because if it was, I got news for you, pal. I don't scare that easily. Seeing my name on a grave does absolutely nothing to shake my confidence. People have been trying to kill me for the last fifteen years. It's just a way of life by now. And I got news for you, I've been up against and hunted down by more dangerous men than you guys are. So this feels just like a walk in the park to me."

"Oh really?"

Recker shrugged again. "Just telling you how it is."

"You got some balls on you, man."

"Wish you had some."

Naylor made a fist and slammed it down on the table. Then he pointed at Recker. "You know what?!"

"What?" Recker calmly asked.

Naylor took a deep breath, then looked around at everyone, calming himself down. "We're not here for a problem."

"Then why are you here?"

"We're here to make some kind of truce with you."

"A truce?"

"Yeah. You leave us alone, we leave you alone, and all this other nonsense can stop. We'll let bygones be bygones."

"Just like that, huh?"

"What about this blowing up buildings to send me messages? What about all the other things you got planned?"

"What about you gunning down our guys just playing pool?"

76

"Listen, we could go on and on with this stuff," Recker said. "Wouldn't do anybody any good."

"You're right. We can at least agree on that. Basically, it comes down to this. We just wanna avoid problems with you guys. We just wanna coexist."

"Just wanna coexist, huh? Your history certainly doesn't seem like that's a high priority for you guys. You've been a wrecking machine everywhere you've been."

"That's made up media hype. We don't wanna hurt nobody."

"So what's this really about?"

"Just what I told you. We just wanna go our own separate ways, everybody does their own thing, nobody bothers nobody, and we all live happily ever after."

As Recker kept the conversation going so his partner could get into position, Haley had long since moved on by now. He had exited the rear of the building across the street and walked in the direction of the car that was sitting on the next street over. There was a small chain-link fence that he had to climb over, but it wasn't too high, so Haley was able to get over it relatively easily. Once he passed a few more buildings, Haley stood along the edge of another building and peeked out onto the street. He looked to his left and saw the car that Recker described. It was still sitting there.

Haley calmly walked across the street, making it

seem like he was just another guy walking around. Traffic wasn't too bad, though there were a few cars passing here and there. Once he got to the other side, Haley walked along the sidewalk, going in the direction of the car. Recker had already told him there were only two men inside, though it was always possible one was hiding in the back seat or was leaning over when Recker passed by. It didn't really matter to Haley though. He kept his hands in his pockets as he walked along, trying to appear as innocent and unassuming as possible.

Haley slowed down his walk a little as he got closer to the car. He kept his eyes focused on the men in the front seat, not wanting to make his move until their heads were turned so they wouldn't see him fly into action. Once he saw the man in the passenger seat turn his head away, Haley rushed over to the car, and pulled on the back door handle, flinging it open. The men in the front seat instantly turned around to see what was going on, only to see a gun staring at them in the face.

"What the hell..."

Haley didn't allow the driver to finish his statement, instead putting two rounds into his chest. The passenger tried to reach for his gun, but it was too late. Haley had already fired at him by the time he put his fingers on his weapon. Both men slumped forward as Haley sat there for a moment, making sure his work was finished.

"One car's been neutralized," Haley said.

"Excellent work, Chris," Jones replied.

"On to the next one."

Haley stepped out of the car and looked around, making sure there were no witnesses. There weren't. He closed the door to the car and slowly started walking away, heading to the next vehicle.

Recker heard Haley was done with the second target, but needed to keep his adversaries talking as long as possible so his partner could finish the job. Recker didn't really care what was being said at that point, as long as he kept them at the table. He figured at most, he only needed to keep them there a few more minutes to give Haley the time he needed.

"So what do you say?" Naylor asked. "Do we have a deal?"

"You really think I buy all this?" Recker replied. "You really think I'm stupid enough to believe that all you want is a truce?"

"What else would we want? Listen, a war between us wouldn't do either side any good. If this thing gets drawn out real long between us, a lot of people are going to get hurt or killed. We don't want that."

"Public-spirited citizens."

"Listen, if it's a war you want, we'll give it to you. We're trying to be nice and give you a lifeline."

"Give me a lifeline? Now who's the funny one?"

"We both know we outnumber you fifty to one. You really wanna continue this? I mean, we'll put you in a box if you do."

"I put the odds a little less than that. Especially after today."

"After today? What's that mean?"

Recker shrugged and shook his head. "Not important."

Naylor smiled. "You believe this guy? We're throwing him a bone and he's got that cocky attitude like he can do no wrong."

"If you don't like my attitude, you can try to do something about it right now."

"Maybe we should."

While all the parties were disarmed before they came in, just in case a problem started, Recker didn't have a problem throwing down if that's what they wanted. He figured he had Malloy in his corner if push came to shove.

"Gentlemen, gentlemen," Vincent said. "Let's calm it down and remain cool. You asked me here to preside over a civilized meeting, not over a brawl fest."

Naylor looked over at him and put up his hands, indicating he would comply. Recker nodded, that he was still willing to keep the peace. Recker continued the conversation for a few more minutes, finally hearing Haley's voice in his ear again.

"Got the second car in my sights."

"How's the situation look?" Jones asked.

"Pretty similar to the first one. Think I can do the same thing."

"Be careful."

It wasn't quite the same situation though. This time, there were three men in the car. That would make getting in a little trickier. But, Haley still thought he could do it. It was either that or start blasting away at them through the windows. The only problem with doing it that way was it was noisier and would draw attention to him. At least if he was inside the car, he wouldn't have onlookers and passersby staring at him as he was firing through a window that was shattering.

Haley approached the car the same way he did the last one. Slowly, methodically, making sure no one would give him a second look or look at him thinking he had bad intentions in mind. It took him several minutes to walk to the car. As he got closer, he could tell the three men were having a conversation. Their heads were turning a lot, their hands were going up and down, and he could see their mouths moving. That was good news for him. It meant they weren't paying attention to anything else.

Once Haley got near the car, he made a mad dash for it, ripping open the back door and hopping in. He withdrew his gun at the same time as he jumped in, plugging the man in the back seat next to him almost instantaneously. As the other two in the front seat turned around to confront him, Haley blasted away at them, hitting them each with one shot. Neither one was dead and was still moving. Haley made quick work of that though. Before either of them was able to remove their guns, Haley put one more bullet into each of them. It was a fatal blow for them both.

With his work done again, Haley looked around for witnesses. Upon seeing it was clear, he got out of the car. He adjusted his clothes and started walking back toward the warehouse, calmly, as if nothing happened. As he walked away, he informed the others of his progress.

"Second car eliminated."

"Excellent," Jones replied.

"Mike, if you can give me a few more minutes, I think I can work myself around to David's position and take out that last car if you want. If you can buy me another five minutes or so, let me know. Fake a cough if you want me to do it and you're able to. Fake a sneeze if it's a no-go."

Recker almost immediately coughed. He wasn't worried about keeping these guys at the table. He had them eating out of the palm of his hand. He could do whatever he wanted to as far as he was concerned. He knew how to push their buttons if he wanted them to get mad; he knew how to engage them; he knew exactly what made them tick. Keeping them occupied for a few more minutes wouldn't be a problem.

"Don't overextend yourself, Mike," Jones said. "If it's getting too hot in there, don't worry about that last car." Recker coughed again, giving Jones his answer. "I take it that means just shut up and get the job done."

Recker coughed again. "Sorry. Must be catching a cold or something."

A few more minutes went by. This time, Haley rushed over to get to the final car, not wanting Recker to be in there too long and stretch himself too thin and make it obvious that he was stalling for something. Haley ran back down the next street over, where he took out the occupants of the first car. He took a peek at the car as he passed it. Nobody had yet to discover what had happened inside it yet. Haley ran to near the end of the street, stopping a couple buildings short of it, then cut in between them, so he could get to Jones' position.

Once Haley came out on the other side of the street, he immediately saw Jones' car. He walked past the car and gave his boss a little wave. Jones grinned and took a hand off the steering wheel and also gave a half-hearted wave, not sure how Haley could have seemed so relaxed after doing what he'd done, and what he was about to do. But he supposed that's why they were CIA agents. Him and Recker were different inside than most people. They didn't get choked up, as nervous, or mind the danger like most people would. They just weren't wired that way. It's also what made them as good as they were.

Jones kept his eyes on Haley as he approached the other vehicle. This one was slightly different for Haley, since it was an SUV. The back windows were slightly tinted, preventing him from really seeing inside. He thought he was going to have to work this one a little differently than the others. As he walked toward the vehicle, Haley took a sound suppressor out of his pocket and put it on the end of his gun. Since he couldn't see inside, he'd have to get a closer look. The only way to do that was to go right up to it. Without hesitation, Haley walked over to the black SUV and knocked on the passenger side window. The men inside were slightly startled to see a man standing there and banging on their window. The passenger rolled the window down.

"What do you want?"

"Uh, sorry to bother you guys, but you can't park here," Haley answered.

"What?"

"This is a bus stop area. There's no parking here."

"Who are you?"

Haley took a quick look in the back, not seeing anyone there. "Oh, I'm just the friendly neighborhood trash man."

The two men inside the vehicle looked at each other, confused, not sure what this guy was talking about. They were starting to think he was just plain crazy. "Trash man?"

Haley took a quick look around to make sure nobody was walking in his direction. He'd wait if there was. But there wasn't. That side of the street was clear. He cleared his throat.

"Yeah, you see, I walk around the streets, disposing

of the trash in the neighborhood. As a matter of fact, I just disposed of the trash sitting in the cars that your friends were supposed to be in."

"What?"

"You know, the guys you had sitting in the next streets over. Those guys? Oh, and the sniper guy that you had in that building over there, waiting for The Silencer to come out? That guy? Remember him?"

The man in the passenger seat immediately grew concerned about what was happening and reached inside his jacket to remove his gun, ready to take care of the situation. Haley beat him to the punch, though. He removed his own weapon, shooting the passenger in the head, then drilling the driver in the chest. Haley took a quick look again to the back of the car, making sure there were no other problems he needed to take care of. It was clean though. He put his gun away, then took another look at his victims. The passenger was slumped over toward the middle where the gear shift was, while the driver's head was resting comfortably on the steering wheel. With his work there done, Haley walked back to Jones' car and gave him the OK sign. Jones nodded at him as Haley walked by. Haley was taking the long way back to his car. He updated Recker on the way.

"Third car now eliminated."

"I must say, you did efficient work, Chris," Jones said.

"Hey, you pay for the best, you get the best."

"I would say once you get back to your car, continue cruising around, just in case more of them have shown up that we haven't spotted yet."

"Will do. Assuming there's nothing else, though, I think it's safe to call today a victory."

9

With their work there seemingly done, Recker started to wrap up his conversation. He was honestly pretty bored with it by now. They were going over the same things over and over again, mostly because of him and trying to string them along to give Haley extra time. But now that Haley was done, so was he.

"OK, I think we've said it all here," Recker said.

"So do we have a deal?" Naylor asked, putting his hand across the table to shake.

Recker looked at his hand. "We do not. I wouldn't make a deal with you if my life depended on it."

Naylor grinned. "It just might."

"Still wouldn't do it. You guys are slimeballs and the only time I would touch you is if I was putting you in the ground."

Vincent continued sitting there silently, watching the two parties, seeing that nothing was accomplished there. He just hoped they would exit as peacefully as when they came in.

"You're on notice," Naylor said. "What happens after this is all on you."

Recker smiled. "You do what you think you can."

Recker then stood up and left the room, escorted by Malloy. They discussed the situation outside as they walked to the exit.

"Be careful out there," Malloy said.

"Nothing to worry about. It's all been taken care of."

"How do you know?"

Recker reached inside his ear and took out his piece, showing it to Malloy. "I got the updates."

Malloy smiled and shook his head. "You were listening the whole time."

"Sure was."

"You were just stalling in there. You were just keeping them busy long enough to give Haley enough time to take them all out, weren't you?"

Recker smirked. "A good assassin doesn't reveal all his secrets, does he?"

Malloy tapped Recker on the shoulder as the two went out the exit and walked towards Recker's car. They stood there for a few minutes, talking until the two Scorpions came out as well.

"You're a dead man," Naylor said, pointing at Recker as they passed by.

"If you're talking about the sniper you got across the street, or the three cars you got stationed around the area, I hope you're not putting too much faith in them."

Naylor's face looked stunned. He looked at his partner, wondering how Recker could have known what they were planning.

Recker nodded. "That's right. I know. Oh, and, uh, that cemetery you were in when that video was shot, you might wanna dig some more graves for your guys. Just thought I'd throw that out there."

Naylor didn't bother responding and just huffed and puffed on his way back to his car. Once the Scorpions were inside their car, they stormed out of the area.

"Chris, Naylor's leaving now. Can you give him a loose tail? They'll know my car if I follow."

"I'm on them," Haley replied.

"Looks like a happy ending," Malloy said.

"For today," Recker said. "Tomorrow's another issue."

Recker got in his car and drove past the gate. He met Jones at a corner parking lot, both sitting in their vehicles next to each other as they talked.

"Seems that went as well as we could have expected," Recker said.

"I would say so. Now, if Chris comes back with another location, we could consider this a heck of a day."

"One thing's for sure, they're not gonna be happy once they realize the damage."

Haley then got on the line. "Looks like they're driving past every vehicle, making sure what you said was true."

"Guess they didn't believe me."

"Just drove past the last one. They're moving on now."

"Stay with them. Not too close though. We've had a good day so far, no need to push it and make it a bad one."

"I'll be on my tip-toes."

"So what do you want to do next?" Jones asked.

"You might as well go back to the office and do your usual thing."

"What about you?"

"I might as well stay out on the streets and cruise around, just in case Chris needs me for anything."

"He can take care of himself."

"I know that. What I'm saying is, there's no use in me going back to the office, and then if he gets their location, then I have to drive out again. I might as well just stay out here and be closer to begin with."

"Makes sense. I've got my tablet already on, so if he stops somewhere, I've got the tracker on and I'll let you know."

"Good deal. As you head back to the office, just periodically let me know where he's at so I can start heading in that direction."

Jones let Recker know the direction that Haley was currently travelling and then the two of them parted ways. About twenty minutes had passed when Recker's phone started ringing. He assumed it was Jones, though up to now he was just providing updates through the earpiece. He looked down at the caller ID and saw that it was Vincent. He thought he knew what the topic would be.

"Miss me already, huh?"

Vincent laughed. "Yeah, I'm not calling for warm pleasantries."

"Are you ever?"

"I just came out of the warehouse and saw police activity down the street. It seems a couple of men were killed inside an SUV while we were having our meeting?"

"Really? No kidding?"

"And then I've heard there was another car found the next street over. The same fatalities inside."

"Wow, that's a coincidence."

Vincent laughed again. "It gets better. There's even another car, on the next street after that, with three more bodies inside. Isn't that something?"

"Man, that's, uh, wow, what are the odds? You know who these guys were?"

"I haven't got the update yet. I was hoping you might be able to tell me."

"How would I know? I was in with you the whole time."

"Well, considering you don't always work alone, I thought perhaps you still might know something."

"Gee, I really don't."

Vincent wasn't mad, but he did seek to hear what really happened. "Truthfully, Mike, let's cut out all the nonsense. Do you know what really happened out there?"

"Well if you want the truth, you left out one part."

"What part is that?"

"The sniper in the building across the street."

"What sniper?"

"Well, he's dead now too," Recker replied. "Guess the cops haven't found him yet."

"There's a sniper? Just who was he trying to hit?"

"I think me. But I guess we can never be sure."

"I take it your partner is responsible for all those... incidents outside."

"I can neither confirm or deny that I have a partner or that he did any such thing."

"Who are the guys in the cars?"

"Scorpions. I had a feeling they were gonna try something. That meeting was nonsense, they just wanted to get me there, so they knew where I was so they could take me out afterwards."

"And you knew that?"

"I had a good hunch. So before the meeting, we cruised around, identified our targets, and then while I was in there, Chris was doing what was necessary."

"That's impressive work in a short amount of time."

"You don't think I'd let just anybody on board our ship, do you?"

"I guess not. Remind me the next time I see him to offer him a job. I could use someone like him."

"I think he's content with where he's at."

"That seems to be the story with you guys."

"Sorry about all the bodies on your doorstep," Recker said. "I hope it doesn't fall on you at all. But, it was their doing."

"It's OK. No need to worry about that. I won't get any blowback for it. I just wish you would have looped me in."

"Well if you wanna be looped in, I'll tell you that they had a car watching me at our last meeting at the diner."

"They did?"

"Yeah. I took care of it though. And then there were four of them playing pool recently. We took care of that too."

"You're a one-man wrecking crew lately, aren't you?"

"Well, it's not just me. But we're trimming down their numbers and we're gonna keep on trimming them down until the count reads zero."

"And how many have you eliminated?"

"Uh, I think that makes fourteen in the last few days."

"That probably takes their numbers to forty, forty-five, something like that."

"That's about what we figure," Recker said. "I meant what I said. I'm going to drive them out of this city."

"I know you will."

"Though I am surprised at how nicely you're playing with them."

Vincent thought for a second before replying. "It's... more advantageous for me to play nice at the present time. Once, and if, the time comes for me to change my tune, believe me, I will do so."

"Will that be before or after I'm finished?"

Vincent laughed again. "Well, I'll tell ya, Mike. You're doing such a good job with things, why should I get in your way?"

They talked for a few more minutes before finally going their separate ways. Recker got a few more updates on Haley's position. He was still driving, looking like he was going out of the city. The Scorpions went past the airport before eventually coming to a stop.

"They might have finally reached their destination," Jones said, giving Recker the address.

"How long's he been stopped for?"

"A few minutes now. I've tried reaching him, but I couldn't get through."

"If he's only been stopped a few minutes, he should be all right. Chris, you good?" Recker asked. They waited for a reply but didn't get one. "Chris, you OK?"

"We might have just lost the signal."

"I'm hoping it's just the signal that we lost."

10

Recker floored it, trying to get to Haley's position as quickly as possible, just in case he ran into trouble and it wasn't a communication issue. Luckily, he wasn't too far behind. It would take about ten more minutes to get to where Haley was. He just hoped that wouldn't be too late.

Haley was out of his vehicle and had just gotten inside the building that the Scorpions he was following entered. There were a few cars around, so he thought they might have been having some kind of meeting. Probably about the meeting they just had with Recker, and about the other dead bodies of their friends. It was being inside the building that was making the communication issue difficult. There was something inside the building blocking the signal.

It was a two story building that they were in, and Haley entered through an upstairs window. The room he entered was pretty empty except for the dirt and dust. There wasn't a single piece of furniture in it. It looked like it hadn't been used in some time. He went over to the door and opened it, anxiously wondering if someone was on the other side or wandering in a hallway. He slowly opened the door and peeked outside, finding a narrow hallway, though luckily there were no live bodies walking in it.

Haley went into the hallway and started wandering around. There were a few other doors that he peeked inside. A few of them actually had furniture in it, a desk here and there, a couch in a couple of them, but none of them were occupied at the moment. For now, Haley was having trouble figuring out what the building actually was. There was no signage in the front, so he assumed whatever it used to be, it wasn't anymore. It didn't seem to be the traditional warehouse type of building. It wasn't big enough for that unless they were only moving small merchandise.

After clearing the entire upstairs, Haley found stairs at the end of the hallway. He cautiously went down the steps, coming to a door at the bottom that led to the first floor. He gently pushed the door open, expecting to find some people when he poked his head out. He was surprised that he didn't. He knew Naylor and the other guy had come in here. They were there. He saw them walk into the building through the front door. Haley doubted they had left already.

Haley snuck onto the first floor, closing the door

behind him softly. He clung to the wall for a few seconds, just analyzing everything that was in his sights. He stuck his ear in the air, trying to listen for a sound. A voice, footsteps, something falling onto the ground, anything that would give him a clue as to where someone was. He didn't hear anything though. He moved away from the wall and started looking through the immediate vicinity. His gun was out, and he was ready to use it if necessary.

After searching around for a few minutes, Haley thought he detected a light coming from the rear of the building. One piece of the wall seemed like it was a little brighter than the surrounding area. Haley started walking in that direction, hoping he'd finally find what he was looking for. As he got closer to it, he also started hearing voices. They were faint, maybe slightly muffled, as he couldn't really make out what they were saying. But there were at least two of them, that much he could tell. He wouldn't have been surprised if there were more though. He assumed there would be.

Haley kept walking toward the area he assumed Naylor and his friends to be, being careful as to not make any noises to announce his presence. He walked with a soft shoe, making sure there was nothing on the floor he could step on that would make a loud noise. He was somewhat surprised he didn't see a guard or a lookout anywhere. It seemed strange that they wouldn't have one. All the bigwigs had a guard at the door to prevent them from being interrupted or surprised by an unannounced guest.

With nothing in his way, Haley kept moving forward. He went over to the plain brown door and listened to what was going on inside. He could still hear the two voices, though they were becoming a lot louder now. Before he had a chance to do anything else, Haley felt something touching the back of his head. He didn't have to look to know what it was. He knew what the barrel of a gun felt like.

"You might wanna drop that gun," a voice from behind said. "And don't do anything stupid."

Haley cursed at himself under his breath, angry that he was stupid enough to let someone sneak up behind him. He knew something didn't seem right, and he went ahead anyway. He complied with the man's wishes and let the gun fall from his hand.

"Hands against the wall."

Haley stretched his arms up against the wall as someone patted him down, removing the extra weapon he had in the back of his belt. They then spun him around. Haley saw five guys staring at him. He took a deep breath, knowing he was in a pickle. One of the Scorpions knocked on the door and opened it, letting Naylor know it was all clear.

"Well, well, well," Naylor said, walking out and seeing Haley standing there. "What do we have here?"

"Who is this guy?" one of the Scorpions asked.

"I was expecting our friend, Mr. Recker to join us. I

must say I'm a little surprised by your appearance. Who are you?"

"Just the friendly neighborhood watch," Haley answered. "Saw some activity going on, figured I'd investigate. You guys own this building?"

Naylor smiled. "Funny. You have Recker's sense of humor. You must work together. Are you his second fiddle?"

"Hey, listen pal, I am nobody's second fiddle."

"Not even a denial of the name. This must be the mysterious other partner that we've heard so much about."

"I'm nobody's partner."

"Oh, don't be so modest. What's your name so we can have it on record?"

Haley shrugged, knowing it didn't really matter, anyway. He knew what was in store for him. A punch to his gut a few seconds later basically confirmed it. Several of the Scorpions then commenced beating on him for a good solid minute, sending Haley slivering down to the ground.

"The other guy's obviously not coming. Let's just end him and get out of here."

One of the Scorpions removed his gun from its holster and pointed it at Haley's head, ready to end the second Silencer's life. Naylor looked on, ambivalently at first. Then, just before one of his men was ready to fire, Naylor grabbed the man's arm and pulled it down.

"Not yet," Naylor said.

"Why not?"

"Because we have an opportunity here."

"What kind of opportunity?"

"We want Recker," Naylor replied. "This is how we'll get him."

"With this guy?"

"If you want to go fishing for the big sharks, you need to use the right kind of bait. Now we have it. So we should use it to the best of our abilities. You use the smaller bait to get the bigger fish."

"I'm nobody's small bait, pal," Haley said, sitting up against the wall.

Naylor smiled. "You have no idea. Put him in the room and tie him up."

The others complied with the orders and grabbed Haley's arms, dragging him into the room and placing him on a chair. They then tied his arms and legs to the chair.

"Now all we have to do is get word to Mr. Recker that we have his friend," Naylor said.

"Why would he come? He'd have to know we're setting something up for him. He's not that dumb."

"Because he won't just sacrifice his friend. He'll want to try and help. That's who he is. He's someone who feels the need to help anyone who's in trouble. Especially his partner."

"Maybe he'll just get a new one."

"They'll both be dead soon. They can have each other again in the place they're going."

They talked for a few more minutes, trying to figure out the best way to let Recker know they had his partner. They eventually settled on a video. They thought it was the best way to get their message across. Plus, it was more jarring and stimulating to see a friend, a partner, sitting there tied up, cuts and bruises on his face. Just hearing it or seeing the words on a piece of paper didn't have quite the same effect. To make it look even more shocking, they worked Haley over a few more times, making sure his face had plenty of cuts, bruises, and blood to show off to the camera. After they were done using Haley's face as a punching bag, they then started to shoot their video. It wasn't a long one. They were careful not to have anyone else on screen other than their prisoner. They made sure to get plenty of close-ups of Haley's face in the twenty seconds that they were shooting.

Haley, though, felt very uncomfortable that he was being used to lure Recker there. He wished they had just killed him to begin with, that way he didn't have to feel bad about being the one who was used to lure his friend into a dangerous situation. He knew the Scorpions were going to kill him, anyway. But he felt awful that Recker would get drawn into it because he made the mistake of getting captured. He was still cursing himself out, wishing that he had come up shooting instead of just dropping his gun. He knew he wouldn't have been able to come out victorious, but at least Recker would have been safe.

"Where should we send it?"

"Same as last time," Naylor answered. "Vincent will know how to get it to him."

"How long are we gonna play all nice-nice with him, anyway? Let's just take them all out at the same time."

"Patience, my friend, patience. We will take care of Vincent when the time is right. First things first, though. First, we get Recker. Then, we take care of anyone else who is employed by him or with him. Then, after we're sure The Silencer and his team are no more, then, then we go after Vincent. And then, everyone Vincent has gone up against before us... we'll make it look like child's play."

"What if you got this figured all wrong? What if Recker really don't show up?"

"Oh, he'll come," Naylor replied. "I'm sure of it. He'll come."

"But what if he don't?"

Naylor then looked at the battered and bruised Haley. "Then I guess we'll just have to kill him and throw him in the river."

11

Recker didn't have to wait for any video to arrive. He was already in the area. He pulled into the lot near the building, finding Haley's car almost immediately. He got out and checked around the vehicle to see if he detected any signs of a struggle. There weren't though. There was nothing on the ground that looked like it might have dropped from someone during a fight, no marks on the car, and even better, no blood. Recker looked through the window and noticed Haley's phone sitting on the passenger seat. He then called Jones.

"David, I'm standing next to Chris' car."

"I assume he's not in it?"

"No, and his phone's in the car."

"That would explain why he haven't heard from him."

"Probably assumed he could still communicate

with his earpiece," Recker said. "Or he saw something and didn't want to risk bringing his phone in case he was caught or something."

"Have you tried the earpiece lately?"

"Yeah, just a few minutes ago. Still nothing."

"Must be some type of interference," Jones said.

"I got a feeling he's in trouble."

"I get the same feeling."

"I'm gonna go inside this building and check it out."

"Should I meet you there?"

"No, I'll be fine. Just keep trying to get him if you can."

Jones wiped his forehead, already feeling the anxiety kick in over not knowing what was going on with one of the team members. Recker went back to his car as he looked the building over. Something was telling him there was trouble inside. He opened the door to his car and opened the glove compartment, taking out a phone and replacing it with his. If he ran into trouble inside, he didn't want any of his contacts being known if they searched through his phone, but he still wanted to have one in case he needed to call for help. This phone was wiped clean of any contacts inside. It was basically just used as a backup or emergency purposes. Recker figured this would qualify.

Recker went around to the back of the building, trying to look into any windows that he could. Most were boarded up or so dirty that looking inside wasn't possible. He saw a fire escape ladder that went up to a second-floor balcony. The hairs on the back of his neck were screaming to him that something evil was lurking inside, but nevertheless, he had to go. If his friend was inside, he didn't care who or what was waiting for him. He was coming. And there was nothing that would stop him. After getting to the second floor, Recker saw the window was open just a crack.

"Convenient."

Recker opened the window further and then climbed in. He immediately took his gun out, thinking he would have to use it soon. He looked around the room he was in, almost expecting someone to jump out at him. There was nothing there though, other than a few crooked paintings on the wall. He moved out into the hallway and checked each room he came across. There was nothing in any of them though. It was like a ghost town up there. He went back into the hallway and moved toward the stairs. He knew that's where he'd find something.

As Recker descended the steps, it suddenly dawned on him that maybe he wasn't walking into a cold reception. All this time, he just assumed that there was trouble waiting for him inside that building. But now, he thought, what if the trouble had already left? What if there was nobody left inside that building? What if the only thing he was going to find was Haley's body? That would explain why they haven't heard from him. Until that moment, Recker never even thought about the possibility of his friend and partner being dead. He couldn't. He just always assumed that no matter what threat they were up against, they would always make it out OK. Maybe not unscathed, but they'd make it out still breathing. What if this was the one time their profession finally caught up to them?

Recker had stopped in the middle of the stairs as he thought about the possibilities, but shook his head to get them out of his mind. He couldn't think like that. Haley was still alive. He had to believe that. Recker kept going down the stairs until he reached the bottom. He slowly opened the door and looked out, still finding nothing. He checked the floor and the walls in his immediate vicinity for blood stains. Luckily there were none.

Just as he was about to move forward, Recker's head snapped to his left, hearing a loud noise. It sounded like a metal object dropping to the floor or a piece of pipe banging against the wall. Whatever it was, it was unmistakable. Someone was there. Recker started walking toward the direction of the noise, holding his gun out in front, figuring he would be using it any second.

As he took a few more steps, Recker saw a shadow moving on the wall. It looked like someone was standing there, beyond the next corner, waiting for him to arrive. Recker thought about reversing course and going a different direction, but he wasn't sure of the layout of the building and whether it actually would lead to him coming up on the other side of the man. He decided to just keep on marching on in the direction he was going.

Once Recker got near the corner that led to the next hallway, instead of walking slowly, he rushed over to the wall, trying to surprise whoever was there by speeding things up. The man that was waiting there looked slightly startled by Recker's presence, but then held up a metal object high above his head and was about to bring it down and strike Recker in the head with it. Recker fired off two rounds, killing the man before he was able to strike. The pipe fell to the ground, clanging around. Recker recognized the man's face as one of the Scorpions.

Recker stepped over the man's body and kept moving forward. Now he knew they were definitely there. And he assumed that wasn't the last surprise that they had in store for him. He wondered when the next one would appear. Recker kept moving down the hallway, both hands on his gun, ready to fire at whoever came into his sights next. He didn't have to wait long. About twenty feet away, a door opened up, and a man jumped out, firing in Recker's direction. The shot missed wide, ricocheting off the wall. Recker dropped to one knee and returned fire, hitting the man in the chest, knocking him onto his back. Recker kept his eyes peeled for anyone else as he walked along, though nothing else was imminent.

Once Recker got to the body, he crouched down,

splitting his focus between the man by his feet and anyone else who may have come along. Recker reached down and put his fingers on the man's neck, feeling for a pulse. There was none. Suddenly, another shot rang out. Recker felt a jolt in the back of his shoulder, an instant pain that could only come from a bullet. Unfortunately, he'd felt that kind of pain before. He was knocked off his feet, rolling forward onto the ground. He then looked back, seeing a couple of men by the edge of the last corner, where he'd killed the first man at. He returned fire, keeping the men at bay for a little while, making them retreat behind the cover of the wall.

Another shot rang out, once again coming from behind Recker. He once again felt that tightness in his side, feeling like someone was trying to squeeze the life out of him. He fell forward onto the ground again, holding his left side. He turned around and returned fire again. Gunfire was suddenly erupting from both sides, causing Recker to slide into the room the second Scorpion had dashed out from.

In pain, Recker slammed the door shut and sat next to it, his back against the wall. There was another door to the side. It was an all glass stained door. Recker stood up and was about to check it out when the glass suddenly shattered due to the bullets from the assault rifle that were going through it. Recker pointed his gun at the opened door, waiting for another target to appear. It didn't take long. The man with the rifle appeared in the opening, quickly getting gunned down at Recker's hands. The man dropped to the ground, his body landing right in between where the glass door used to be.

Another man appeared in the door, him and Recker exchanging fire almost instantaneously. Both men dropped to the ground after getting hit. The bullet that hit Recker grazed his forearm, causing him to drop his gun briefly. He reached down to pick it up when he heard a voice.

"Don't do it or you're dead!"

Recker looked up at the door, seeing another rifle pointed straight at him. Recker thought of how he could escape this problem, though he didn't see a way out. The man had him cold. The other door opened up, a few more men rushing inside. Suddenly, before he even knew what happened, six men had guns pointed straight at Recker. Assuming this was it for him, he stood up straighter, waiting for his final moments to be over. Then, one of the men stepped aside, letting Naylor make an appearance. He puffed on a big cigar, blowing smoke into the air. He had a wide grin on his face, obviously pleased at the results of their plan. Naylor didn't even care that they'd lost a few more men in the process. Capturing Recker was worth it, and probably would have been worth losing a few more if they had to.

"Well, well, well, the big bad Silencer." Naylor looked at the blood coming from Recker's numerous holes. "Looks like you're not having as good a day as you thought you were, huh?"

Recker shrugged. "It could always be worse."

"After this morning's activities, you were probably feeling pretty sure of yourself, weren't you? Like you were on cloud nine. Like you could do no wrong. Like you were untouchable. Right?"

"I was feeling pretty good," Recker said, trying to make light of things.

"Well that's all changing now, isn't it?"

"Maybe."

"See, we've already got your buddy. Now we got you too. A matching set."

"How nice for you."

"So now what we're gonna do is have a little sit down and talk."

"Eh, I'm not really up for talking," Recker said. "Talking's overrated."

"I think you'll like this one."

"I kind of doubt it. Listen, if you're gonna kill me, which I know you are, just hurry up and get it over with. Why draw it out? Just do it."

Naylor laughed. "You'd like that wouldn't you? No, what we're gonna do, is sit you in a room with your partner, then you're gonna tell us who else is working with you."

"Wasting your time. I work alone."

"See, I know that's not true. You can't. You couldn't

have done all that stuff this morning if you worked alone. You have help."

"No, see what happened was this. I drove around before you got there, noticed all these guys sitting around, then when I saw you go in, then I went around to each one individually and took them out. When that was done, then I went inside with you to have that little wonderful chat we had."

"You're lying."

Recker shrugged, not really having anything else to say. He knew Naylor wasn't going to buy anything he was selling. He was also trying to block out all the pain after having been shot three times. Luckily, none of them were life threatening. At least initially. Considering nobody in front of him looked all that interested in stopping the bleeding, it was always possible he'd just lose too much and pass out. But he wasn't there yet. He was more concerned about the back of his shoulder, mostly because he couldn't see it. The bullet that hit his side, though he couldn't check, didn't feel too bad. It was more of just a burning sensation. And the one that hit his arm just grazed him. The one in his shoulder, though, that felt like it was still in there.

"You're gonna do this the hard way?" Naylor asked.

"I don't know what you want me to tell you," Recker replied. "I don't work with anybody. I mean, I can give you a few made-up names, but that's not gonna do anything for you."

Naylor motioned to the other men to take their prisoner away. "Put him in the room with his friend."

Before doing that, the men went over to Recker and started throwing haymakers. Recker tried to defend himself the best that he could, but considering his injuries, and the fact that there were so many of them, there wasn't much he could do but take the beating. The Scorpions figured Recker would give them problems if they let him walk to the room on his own. Carrying him after eating a couple hundred punches and kicks would make him much easier to deal with.

Once the Scorpions were done with their assault, they picked Recker up, one man on each side of him, and carried him to the same room they were holding Haley in. When the door opened, Haley saw his friend being brought in and put on a chair next to him, though there was still a few feet of space in between them. They didn't want them that close.

"Sorry, man," Haley said, still a little sore and weary from his own beating.

Recker groggily looked over at him. "Hey. At least you're still alive. I was having some doubts about that."

"Only for the moment."

Once the men were finished tying Recker to the chair, they left the room, leaving the two prisoners alone.

"I really screwed up on this one," Haley said.

"I didn't do too much better myself."

"I don't know how we're getting out of this one."

"Be careful what you say," Recker said. "I wouldn't be surprised if they're listening to what we say, hoping we give someone else up."

"There's no one else to give up."

"I know, but they think there is."

They were careful not to mention Jones' name. No matter what happened to them, they weren't going to talk. Part of their training at the CIA was techniques in how to withstand torture punishment. There was nothing the Scorpions could do to them that would make them give up their friend. They would both die first. In fact, they both assumed that was what their fate would be, anyway. And if that was the case, then they both wanted Jones to remain safe so he could continue on with what they had started. If they didn't make it out of this situation, and it didn't seem like they would, they wanted Jones to keep on with the operation and find a couple more men or women that he could trust and rely on as much as them.

"How you feeling?" Recker asked.

"Probably better than you. And that's saying something. You look like shit."

"I feel worse. You shot or anything?"

"No. They just put me through the meat grinder with their hands."

"I got the same treatment. After they shot me a few times."

"How bad?"

"I think two just grazed me." Recker struggled and

tried to move his shoulder, in a little more pain now that it was being restrained and in an uncomfortable position. "One's in the back of my shoulder. That's not feeling too pleasant right now."

"I bet. So what do you think they're waiting for?"

"I think they're waiting for one of us to crack."

"They'll be waiting a long time," Haley said.

"I know. They don't know our background, so they assume we're just a pair of regular guys, probably."

"How are we gonna get out of this?"

"I don't know," Recker answered. "Best I can figure is if they happen to untie one of us for some reason, we rush them, take one of their guns, and then start blasting away. Probably get killed in the process but at least it'll be over with."

"I got a feeling they're not untying us anytime soon."

"Yeah, probably not."

"And even if they do, I don't think either of us are moving too quick right now."

"Well, unless we can somehow wriggle loose here, I think that's about the best we can do."

"Should I start praying for miracles?"

Recker tried to laugh through the pain. "I'm pretty sure miracles left us a long time ago."

12

ecker and Haley were left to themselves for about twenty minutes before the door opened up again. Naylor was the first one through it, with several of his buddies right behind him. He held up the phone he took off of Recker before he was brought in.

"So is there a secret code for cracking this or something?"

"Yeah," Recker said. "Type in 8675309. That should get you in."

Naylor held the phone up. "Not a single contact, phone number, text message, anything. There's nothing in here."

"I'm not a popular guy."

Naylor laughed. "You expect me to believe that?"

"Doesn't really matter to me."

"Why don't you just make it easy on yourselves

and give up the other people that you're working with? You can save yourself a lot of pain if you do it now."

"Being in pain's overrated."

"Well you're gonna feel a lot of it."

"Bring it on."

Naylor looked at one of his cohorts, a bigger man, who walked over to Recker, and proceeded to punch him in the face a few times. It opened up a cut over Recker's left eye. The man then put pressure on Recker's injured shoulder, causing him to wince in pain, though he tried to keep himself under control.

"How much of this do you wanna sustain?" Naylor asked.

"However much you wanna dish out. When are you gonna get to the torture part?"

Naylor laughed, appreciating Recker's sense of humor. It was too bad they were on opposite sides, he thought. Recker would have made a great asset to the Scorpions. Naylor had no thoughts about even trying to turn Recker to the other side. He knew that would be an illusion that wasn't possible. He let his associate throw a few more haymakers on Recker's face, then let the same thing happen to Haley, not wanting to leave him out of the festivities.

"Do you guys really wanna go through this for a few more hours?"

"Why, afraid of hurting your hands?" Recker asked with a laugh.

"I don't think they got the energy to keep this up for a few more hours," Haley said.

Naylor had a smug expression on his face as he looked at the two of them. He did admire their humor as they faced a certain death. After a few more minutes, Naylor finally called off his men.

"That's enough for now. We'll give them some time to think about their futures for a little bit. Give them a little time to recuperate until the next round."

"We going old-school?" Recker asked. "Fifteen rounds?"

"I don't think you could handle fifteen rounds."

"Listen, Sally, I can go all night long. Afraid I'll outlast you?"

"Never stops with you, does it?"

"Am I irritating you yet?"

"Not at all," Naylor replied. "I just hate to go through all this and put you in so much pain when I'm gonna get what I want eventually, anyway. Do yourselves a favor. Just come clean so we can put you out of your misery. Unless someone else is coming of course."

"There's nobody else," Recker said.

"So you say."

"It's true," Haley said.

"I know for a fact there was a third guy at the hospital with you."

"He was shot. Didn't make it."

"That's right," Recker said. "Died on the way out of there."

"A likely story, but I'm afraid one that I don't quite believe."

"Suit yourself. If you wanna waste your time, go ahead."

Naylor and his men, realizing they weren't going to get anything extra out of their prisoners at the current time, then left the room again. They planned to keep going through this routine for as long as it took. They figured, eventually, Recker and Haley would break down. They definitely were a tough pair to crack, but everybody had their breaking point. It just might take some time to reach theirs. But the Scorpions believed they would get there at some point. And they were ready for the long haul. Whether that took twelve hours, all day, or a couple of days, they would get the information they were seeking. They were sure of that.

Once the Scorpions left the room, Recker and Haley looked at each other, though it was tough to see with the blood that was streaming down both of their faces. Considering their arms were tied, it was kind of uncomfortable. Still wary of the Scorpions listening from another room, they were careful not to say anything that would give Jones away. But secretly, they were both hoping Jones had some type of plan that would get them out of there. That was mostly their plan in trying to egg their captures on in trying to continue the beatings. The longer it took, the more time it gave Jones to figure out a way to extract them. They figured they could hold out for a few days. There was nothing the Scorpions could do to them that they hadn't been through before in training. Some of those methods were extreme. They doubted the Scorpions could match it. But they weren't eager for them to try either.

Another twenty minutes went by, and then the Scorpions entered the room again. It was the same song and dance routine as before. Nothing new or different, and Recker and Haley didn't say anything new or different. The punches weren't new or different either. After they were done, the Scorpions left the room again, leaving the two men to their own morbid thoughts about their future.

"How long before they finally realize they're not getting anything and give up?" Haley asked.

"I think when they finally decide to give up they'll kill us."

"Well... at least we have something to look forward to."

Recker's thoughts turned to Mia. He hated thinking that he may never see her pretty face again. He knew it would be rough on her if they had seen each other for the last time. He just hoped that she would forgive him for living the life that he did and that she would eventually find happiness again with someone else. His thoughts of Mia were interrupted when Naylor came through the door again.

"Earlier than usual this time," Recker said. "Changing up your patterns now?"

Naylor smiled, still appreciating the humor. "No, see, I like to consider myself a patient man. And my plan was to wait this out as long as it takes. But... I'm not a patient man. And I'm tired of waiting. So we're gonna speed this process up now."

"Oh, you finally gonna leave for good?"

"No, I'm gonna make one of you talk."

"Not happening, Suzy."

"We'll see about that."

Naylor motioned to one of his men, who took a pistol out of his pocket. The man with the gun then walked around the backs of both Recker and Haley. He then pressed the gun against Haley's temple. Haley closed his eyes, waiting for the man to squeeze the trigger. The man took the gun away from Haley and walked over to Recker, putting it on the back of his head. Recker looked at Naylor, thinking this was some kind of ploy to get them nervous and make them talk. Recker wasn't buying it though. But if he was wrong, and Naylor wasn't fooling around, he didn't look nervous or scared. Recker had accepted that this was his probable fate a long time ago, even back when he was in the CIA. This was usually how it ended for guys like him. A bullet in the back of the head.

Naylor was reading the faces of his prisoners as the gun was placed on their head, judging their reactions. He was going to kill one of them first. The other was going to be made to talk. The one that looked less nervous about dying, he was the one who was going to be the first victim. That was Recker. Naylor believed that even if they killed Haley, Recker still wouldn't be an easy nut to crack. It might take days, if ever, before he finally decided to reveal anything.

Naylor wasn't sure Haley would be that easy either, but he thought he wouldn't be quite as tough as his partner. If he was wrong, well, they were both going to die anyway, so picking incorrectly wouldn't be a big deal. Naylor then looked at his associate and pointed at Haley. The man with the gun then walked around to the front of Haley and stared down at him. He then walked over in front of Recker and raised his gun at Recker's head.

"I'm sorry it had to come to this," Naylor said. "But I'm sure you understand."

"What are you doing?" Haley asked, getting nervous.

"Oh, you see, I'm tired of playing games. Maybe if one of you sees the other one get shot right in front of you, maybe you'll be more receptive to talking."

"You tell him nothing," Recker said, still defiant as ever.

Naylor shook his head. "Always the stubborn one, huh? Right down to the very end. Any last words you would like to say?"

Recker took a deep breath. "Chris, it's been a pleasure working with you."

"Likewise," Haley replied.

Recker looked at Naylor, then the man with the

gun. "Well, get on with it, don't just stand there all day."

"You wanna see it coming?" the man asked.

"Don't matter. Do whatever you want."

The man walked around to the back of Recker's chair. He raised his gun up, pointing it at Recker's head. Haley started to watch, but he couldn't. He just stared straight away, waiting to hear that awful sound to let him know it was over. The man with the gun then looked at Naylor, waiting for the final call. Naylor was just about to give it when gunfire erupted in the main part of the warehouse.

"What's that?" the man with the gun asked.

Naylor rushed out the door to see what was happening, the man with the gun following. Haley looked over at his partner, thanking they got some extra time.

"Looks like you got a reprieve."

"Only temporary I'm sure," Recker said.

"Wonder what's going on out there?"

"I dunno. You can bet it's not David though. Those shots came from assault rifles. More than one. David and assault rifles do not go hand in hand."

"Maybe it's the cops," Haley said.

"Great. Go from one fire to another."

"Hey, even if it is the cops, we still got that pass from Lawson."

"That's true. I'd still prefer not to use it if necessary."

"Right now I'd take any lifeline we can get. Just throw us that life raft and I'll take it."

The gunfire stopped after five minutes. It was eerily quiet for Recker and Haley, not knowing what was going on. They heard what sounded like feet shuffling around, and then voices, on the other side of the door. Their hearts started pounding, expecting Naylor and his cohorts to come back in and finish what they started.

"Hey, if you get out of this and I don't," Recker said. "I want you to tell Mia that I love her."

"You'll tell her yourself."

"Tell her that I'm sorry."

"You got nothing to..."

"And tell her that I want her to move on, eventually."

Haley sighed, not wanting to deliver a message like that. But he finally nodded that he would. "Yeah."

A few more minutes went by, Recker and Haley's eyes both glued to the door, waiting for it to open. It finally did after another two or three minutes. One man stood there. He was dressed in black, had an assault rifle in his hands, and a black mask over his face, except for the part that was cut out for his eyes. Neither Recker or Haley recognized the figure at first. Then, the man reached his hand up to his face and put it on the mask, slowly taking it off his head. The man had a smile on his face as he looked at Recker and Haley.

"Somebody call the rescue squad?" Malloy asked.

Recker and Haley looked at each other and started laughing. They now knew, somehow, they made it out of another one. A couple more masked men came in the room and went over to the two men sitting in the chairs and untied them.

"You guys done fooling around here now?" Malloy joked.

Recker slowly moved his arms around after they were free, trying to get the range of motion back. "Thanks."

Malloy noticed the blood around Recker's shoulder. "We better get you to a doctor."

"I got one."

"She working right now?"

"Yeah."

"Ours will be faster. And it doesn't look like you should be waiting any longer."

"How'd you know we were here?" Haley asked, standing up once he was no longer restrained.

Malloy looked at the both of them as he answered. "Got a call from a certain third party." Recker and Haley instantly knew who that was. "Right about the same time, we got some video sent to us with you being worked over."

"Vincent know you're here?" Recker asked.

Malloy nodded. "He does. He said just make sure I'm not caught, recognized, or dead. I'd like to think I accomplished all three."

"Naylor dead?"

"Must have slipped out the back. Looks like we knocked off eight of them though. Not a bad day's work between the two of us."

"What about you guys? Any casualties?"

"Looks like one." Malloy then looked at Haley a little more closely. "You should probably see the doc too. Looks like they used your face for hamburger meat."

Haley smiled. "Feels a little better now."

"Can you guys walk out of here or you need me to wheel in the wheelchairs?"

"We can manage," Recker replied.

As they walked out the door, Haley put his hand on Recker. "Guess it's a good thing I prayed for that miracle after all."

Recker smiled. "Yeah. Guess we still had one left in us at that."

13

Recker and Haley had just finished getting patched up by Vincent's doctor. By the time they exited the office, Vincent had now joined Malloy in waiting for them.

"You two almost look less than decent," Malloy said, getting a laugh from the two men being worked on.

"Almost," Haley replied.

"So what's the verdict?" Vincent asked.

"I'm fine," Haley answered. "Might just take a little while for some of these cuts and bruises to heal."

"And you?" Vincent asked, looking at Recker.

"I'm ready to go again," Recker said.

Vincent took a careful look at Recker, not noticing any obvious signs of him being shot, other than a small bandage on his forearm.

"You look remarkably well for a man who's been shot."

"I got lucky," Recker said. "Low-powered bullet, didn't hit any bones, just gotta try and take it easy for a bit."

"We all know how that will go."

"We'll see."

Recker was in a little worse shape than he let on, and in a little pain, but he wasn't going to show it. Not there. Besides the bandage on his arm, he also had one on his side and one on the back of his shoulder. The shoulder wound was the one he had to be careful about. Though it didn't hit any major organs, muscles, or bones, he was still advised to keep it as still as possible for the next few weeks. Recker wasn't sure how well he was going to be able to follow those directions with the Scorpions still on the loose. And with them taking a massive number of casualties, now was still the time to strike. Luckily, the wounded shoulder wasn't his shooting arm. Though he was able to shoot with both hands, and his off-hand, his left, was still better than most people's best, he was still more comfortable shooting right-handed.

"What are your plans from here?" Vincent asked.

"Same as before," Recker answered. "Get rid of them when the opportunity is there."

Vincent nodded, thinking of his options. "We may have an opportunity now."

"How so?"

"By my count they've lost, what, seventeen men?"

"Sounds about right."

"We should strike while the iron is hot."

"We?!"

"I believe the time is right for me to get involved now."

"No offense, but why?"

Vincent smiled. "Let's just say the numbers are more to my liking now."

Recker looked at him curiously, wondering what his motive was now. But, he wasn't going to ask a lot of questions. They needed all the help they could get, especially now.

"Don't misunderstand my lack of action before as being weak or stupid," Vincent said. "I know full well that the Scorpions always have intended to dispose of me after going after you. But I always strike when the time is right for me. No one else."

"Why is now that time?"

"Their numbers are lower, they're probably questioning themselves, morale for them is low, and I think I can use my position to lure them deeper. Plus, judging by the faces of you two, it looks like you could use the help."

"You have something in mind?" Recker asked.

"I do."

"You gonna share?"

"When the time is right. Let's just say... I should be able to leverage my position, as someone with the power to get things done, and they're burning hatred for you, in order to set something up."

"Let me know when that happens."

"I will do so. In the meantime, Jimmy will take you back to your vehicles, unless you preferred going straight to your homes or office?"

Recker smiled. "Our cars will be fine."

"Fine. Hopefully, you won't have to get through any police tape to get to them."

They said goodbye to Vincent, then followed Malloy out to his car. Once inside and on the road back to their vehicles, Recker was curious whether Malloy knew anything about his boss' plan.

"You know what Vincent is planning?"

Malloy shook his head. "Hasn't told me yet."

"Is that the truth or is that the company line?"

Malloy looked at him and grinned. "The truth. I don't know how long he's been thinking about it. Maybe he's had it in mind all the time, or maybe he just thought of it while he was waiting for you guys to get checked out. I don't know. I'm sure he'll tell me when he wants to set it up."

"Sounds like he's got an ambush in mind," Haley said. "Like maybe he's going to try to broker another meeting, and then once he's got them in sight, open fire."

"Possible. If I know him, it's probably a little more involved than that. A regular meeting would only involve one or two men. If he's setting something up, he'll want to take out at least a dozen if not more."

"Why do you think he wants to get involved now?" Recker asked.

"My guess? He sees the opportunity to end this quickly. He doesn't want to get into another long, drawn-out war with someone. But we can all see they're reeling right now. They're ripe for another takedown."

They continued talking about Vincent's possible plans, throwing a lot of theories around, until they finally arrived back at the building they were previously at. Surprisingly, there were no police cars around yet. It had been about two hours since they were there last, but it wasn't in a heavily populated area, so it was possible no bystanders were around to call in the trouble. Or maybe no one heard the trouble. In any case, it was easier for them that the police weren't there yet. Recker and Haley got out of the car, but before going back to theirs, had a few more questions for their driver.

"So I'm assuming David was the one who called you?"

"That's right," Malloy answered. "He called me, said Haley went missing, then you went missing, gave me the location of the building. Then as I was about to leave, we got a video from them with Haley's lovely face on it. So I told Vincent, said we needed to help, he approved it, said just make sure I'm covered head to toe and to make sure nobody knows it's us doing the rescuing. The rest you know."

"Well... thanks. Guess we owe you one."

Malloy shrugged. "You've helped me out of a few tough jams if I remember right."

"We even now?"

"Who's keeping track?"

Malloy drove off, then Recker and Haley got in their cars, quickly getting out of the area before anyone else showed up. Once they got back to the office, Recker and Haley talked for a few minutes behind the building before going up to see Jones.

"What are you gonna do about Mia?" Haley asked.

Recker sighed. "I don't know."

"There's no way you're gonna be able to hide all that from her. Not for a few weeks."

"Well, the cuts and bruises I can explain."

"You're not gonna have full range of motion in that shoulder for a couple weeks."

Recker sighed again, just picturing the conversation he and Mia would have. "I know."

"You gonna tell her exactly what happened?"

"Well, we made an agreement a long time ago to never lie to each other. But this might be one of those times when... maybe I can tell her I was hit with an errant bullet while you were cleaning your gun or something."

Haley laughed. "She'd never believe that. She knows I wouldn't be that careless."

"Yeah. Well, I guess I'll just tell her the truth."

"The whole truth?"

"Well, just the part that matters."

"Isn't that all of it?"

"Well, I'll just say we got into a battle with the Scorpions and I took a bullet. She doesn't need to know we were captured and came within minutes of getting killed. She can deal with the first part. The second part... the second part would require a much longer conversation I think."

"How long before the real conversation happens?" Haley asked.

"Which one is that?"

"The one where she wants you to do something safer."

Recker looked out at the bushes behind the building. "It's probably coming soon."

"How are you gonna handle that?"

"Same way I always do. Just play it by ear."

Once they were finished talking, they climbed the steps and went into the office. Jones was sitting at his desk typing away, though he saw them pull into the parking lot on one of the monitors.

"Took you long enough to come in," Jones said. "What were you doing out there?"

"Just talking," Haley answered.

"I gathered that."

Jones spun his chair around to look at his two friends, getting an up front view of the damage they sustained. He couldn't remember a time when their faces looked as bad as it did now.

"Well you two are a sight for sore eyes."

"Thanks," Recker said. "We feel great too."

"No sling for the shoulder?"

Recker slightly moved it. "No, it's fine."

"That's not what the doctor says."

"The doctor? You talked to the doctor?"

"I did."

"What, you have him on speed dial now?"

"Vincent gave me his number. I thought it would be beneficial to hear it straight from the horse's mouth so to speak."

"Since when are doctors supposed to be speaking about a patient's health to unauthorized people?"

"Mike, we're dealing with an underground doctor," Jones said. "Albeit a very sophisticated and surprisingly good one, who actually has sterile equipment, but still, one who's not really bound by the normal oaths."

"An oath's an oath. They should stand by it, regardless."

"Be that as it may, you're supposed to take it easy for the next few weeks."

"He said two to three probably," Recker said. "That means I should be back to normal in one."

Jones shook his head. "Always pushing the envelope."

"I'm in good shape. I heal faster than most people."

"More stubborn than most people too."

"It's gotten me to where I am."

"It's gotten you to a bullet in your shoulder."

"I'll be fine."

"Yes, thankfully, but what do you think Mia will say when she sees you? Do you think she's going to let you go out all half-cocked like that?"

"I don't do anything half-cocked."

"You know full well what I mean."

"I know, I know. Everyone's concerned and I appreciate it. But I'll be fine."

"The question isn't whether you'll be fine, but whether you need to take a week or two off."

"Not possible right now."

Jones looked away and sighed. "Michael, now is not the time to be stubborn. There's too much at stake."

"I agree, there is. So stop fighting me."

"What are you going to do out there with one arm?"

Recker pulled out his gun and pointed it at the wall, pretending like he was going to fire. "See? I only need one arm to shoot."

Jones closed his eyes and shook his head. He knew this was yet another battle that he was not going to win. He then looked at Haley for help.

"Maybe you can try."

"I dunno," Haley said, not really helping Jones' position. "Maybe instead of trying to keep him on the sidelines, we can figure out what he can still do to help in his current position, while still protecting him at the same time."

Jones lifted his hand up, then let it slap against his knee. "Now there's two of them."

Recker pointed his hand at Haley, agreeing with his point of view. "There you go. Spoken like someone who's got his head in the game."

"OK, OK," Jones said. "Do what you want. I know you will anyway. I just hope you don't do something stupid and get yourself killed. I really don't want to be the one who has to console Mia and deliver the bad news."

"You won't have to. I'm not gonna do something stupid or that I'm not capable of doing. Even if that means letting Chris take the lead and I backup, or I use myself as a decoy, something, I can't just sit on the sidelines for this. We can't afford it."

"May not matter anyway," Haley said.

"Why is that?" Jones asked.

Haley looked at Recker. "Tell him about Vincent."

Recker then proceeded to tell Jones what Vincent said, about joining in the fray.

"What do you make of that?" Jones asked.

"Don't know. But whatever it is, I doubt we'll have long to wait."

"What makes you think so?"

"Because if Vincent's getting involved, it means he already has a plan. And it means he'll do it soon."

14

By the time Recker got home that evening, Mia was already at the apartment waiting for him. He hadn't yet told her about what happened, figuring that was news better to be said in person. If he said it in a text or a phone call, she'd probably still worry, wondering if it was really worse than what he was telling her because he didn't want her to be upset. But if he waited to do it in person, she could see that he was all right.

Before he walked in the door, Recker took a deep breath, knowing he was going to have a lot of explaining to do. He just hoped that Mia didn't freak out, not that he would have blamed her if she did, but he hoped she remained as calm as she usually did. Recker unlocked the door and went in, surprised that he didn't see his girlfriend right away. He then heard her moving around in the kitchen, closing a few cabinets.

"Mia?"

Mia came rushing out of the kitchen to greet her boyfriend. "Hey," she said, turning the corner and looking at him. Any other thoughts in her head completely disappeared when she saw him. She stood there, paralyzed, her mouth falling open, unable to process what she was seeing. She couldn't ever remember seeing him look as beat up as he did.

"Oh. My. God." Mia then walked over to him. "What... happened... to you?"

Recker let out a laugh. "You should see the other guy."

Mia gently put her hands on his face and rubbed some of his wounds. "What happened?"

"It's a long story."

"Well you're gonna tell me about it."

Mia then touched Recker's injured shoulder, causing him to wince. Her eyes opened wide, knowing there was more to the story than just his face. She tried to put her hand on his shoulder again, but Recker pulled back. Mia put her hands on her face, covering her nose and mouth, as she just looked at him.

"You've been shot, haven't you?"

Recker made a face like she was crazy for thinking it. "Why would you say that?"

"You have, haven't you?"

"Why is that the first thing you assume?"

"Because I know better."

"Maybe I just got hit with something..."

"Like a bullet?"

"No, like someone dropped a hammer on me, or I walked into a tree, or I was lifting weights and pulled a muscle. Why do you always assume the worst?"

"Because I know you."

Recker sighed and shook his head. He was too easy to figure out.

"You have been shot, haven't you?"

Recker closed his eyes, looking disgusted that he actually had to admit it. He finally nodded. Mia's hands rose up to the top of her head, running her fingers through her hair. She looked him up and down, watching for any other signs of injury.

"Is that it?" Mia asked, not seeing anything else that was obvious. She knew with him though, that he could have been trying to mask a thousand other injuries.

"Umm, no, that's basically it."

Mia tilted her head to the side. That was a dead giveaway he was hiding more. If that truly was it, he would have answered much more decisively.

"Mike, just tell me."

"Ahh, it's nothing." He then rolled up his sleeve and revealed the bandage on his forearm. "Just a little scrape is all."

"And what's that from?"

"Uh, you know, just a metal object that went by."

Mia laughed, though not out of amusement. It was

mostly at how her boyfriend described getting shot. "A metal object? Like a bullet?"

"Yeah, but it basically missed. No big deal. Hardly even feel it." Recker then gave her a smile, hoping she'd calm down. He could tell she was starting to get worked up.

Mia took a deep breath, hoping that was everything he was dealing with. She reached up and kissed him softly on the lips, putting her hands on his hips. As she did, she thought she detected him squirming ever so slightly. She pulled away to face him again.

"Is there something else?"

Recker shook his head. "Nope. What else would there be?"

"I thought you moved kind of different when I kissed you."

"Just my face hurt."

"No, that wasn't it."

"I would know, wouldn't I?"

"You also don't want me to worry and try to hide things."

"I'm fine."

Mia didn't believe a word of it and instead lifted up his shirt. She closed her eyes for a second, disappointed, when she saw another bandage on his side.

"Mike..."

"Everything's fine."

"How can you say everything's fine?" Mia asked. "Your face has at least ten cuts on it, you're shot in three different places, you got bandages everywhere, how can you say things are fine?"

"Because I'm not dead?"

Mia took another deep breath. "That's not reassuring. And it's not funny either."

"I say everything's fine because it is. I'm not hurt too bad. I can walk, talk, eat, all those good things."

Mia grabbed his arm and led him over to the couch. "Let's sit over here so we can go over everything."

"There's really not much to go over."

"Yeah, right. I don't believe that. You're gonna tell me everything or you're sleeping by yourself for the next month."

Recker's eyes hit the floor, not really liking either proposition. He still debated on how much he should tell her, knowing she would really be upset if he told the whole truth. He eventually decided on just telling her most of it, leaving out the part about being tied up in a chair. Mia sat there quietly for a few moments, trying to process everything. Something wasn't quite sitting right with her though. It wasn't making total sense to her.

"Wait, something's not adding up here. How did you get those cuts and bruises on your face again?"

"Like I said, Chris and I got into a fight with them after they started shooting. Pretty simple."

Mia squinted her eyes at him, still thinking something was fishy. She scratched her cheek as she thought. "So how were you able to throw punches after you were shot?"

Recker shrugged with his good shoulder. "Just moving on adrenaline I guess."

Mia stared at him for a few moments, trying to read his face. "You're lying. I can tell."

"I'm not."

"You are. There's something you're trying to avoid telling me. I can always tell when you're lying to me. You're not very good at it. You speak to me in a different way when you're lying."

"What way?"

"It's just different. I can tell. I'm not gonna say specifically because then you'll try to change it and fool me."

"Really?"

"You would," Mia said. "Now tell me the real story."

"I've already told you the real story."

Mia nodded, then got up. She went over to her purse and removed her phone. Recker looked at her curiously, wondering what she was doing. Mia held the phone up.

"Are you going to tell me the real story now?"

"I already did," Recker answered.

"OK." She then started dialing the phone.

"What are you doing?"

"I'm calling Chris. I'm gonna ask him what happened and see if his story matches yours."

Recker looked away and cursed at himself.

"Damn." He didn't anticipate his girlfriend pulling this move and didn't bother to coordinate stories with Haley to make sure they matched.

"Should I continue?"

Recker let out a large audible sigh, then shook his head. "No."

"You gonna tell me the truth now?"

Recker closed his eyes and nodded. "Yeah."

Mia then went back over to the couch and sat down next to him, impatiently waiting for him to begin. She was tapping her foot and fiddling with her fingers as she waited to hear the real truth. Recker cleared his throat, then relayed the day's events, starting with the meeting with the Scorpions at Vincent's warehouse. He remembered every little detail and didn't try to hide a thing, even the part about being tied up. Mia was nervously fidgeting her body around as he explained everything, almost as if it was still happening and still had something to be nervous about. A couple of times she put her hand over her mouth, partly in shock, and partly so she didn't say something and interrupt him, wanting to hear the entire story. Recker didn't look at her much as he recalled everything. Part of it was not wanting to see the worried look in her eyes that he knew she'd have.

"That's it," Recker said, after finishing the story. "That's all of it."

Mia had her hands over her mouth and nose again, the tips of her fingers almost up to her eyes as she horrifically listened to the rest of the story. She could hardly believe it. She didn't even know what to say at that point. She was too stunned to speak. Recker looked at her, waiting for the hammer to fall on him, surprised that she wasn't laying into him. Seeing that she was shocked, Recker put his hand on her arm.

"You OK?"

Mia finally took her hands off her face. "No, I'm not OK! I can't believe all that! I mean, and, you just... you just... act like nothing happened."

"Because nothing did happen... really. Everyone's fine, nobody's hurt. Everything's good."

Mia closed her eyes and shook her head. She really wanted to take a heavy object and hit him on the head with it. Maybe it would knock some sense into him and make them live in the same world.

"No. No, everyone is not fine. Everything is not good. I don't understand why you would think it is. Mike, you were almost killed."

"But I wasn't."

"So, what, another five minutes and you would've been dead?"

Recker shrugged, as if it were no big deal. "Mia, worrying and getting upset over what might have happened, could have happened, should have happened, that's a pointless exercise that will lead you nowhere. You can't worry about that."

"Except for the next time it happens when it really does happen and you leave me for good."

"That's not gonna happen."

"You can't possibly say that and mean it. You don't know. And it can happen."

Recker couldn't argue the point and say that it couldn't. It would be disingenuous to Mia to pretend that it wouldn't. She was smarter than that, anyway. Mia was silent for a minute, trying to collect her thoughts and not sound like an irrational girlfriend. But maybe now was the time for the big talk. The one that they always tried to avoid. The one they both knew was coming.

"Mike, you know I'm not someone who nags you and is hysterical about what you do."

"And I appreciate that."

"But, I mean, how much longer are you going to do this?"

"Mia, it's..."

"No, no, I don't wanna argue about it, I don't wanna give ultimatums, I don't wanna fight, I don't want any of that. But at some point, hopefully before you're killed in some dark alley or warehouse somewhere, we're going to have to talk about our future."

"You thinking about walking out?"

"No. I would never do that. I love you too much for that. I would never walk away from you. But at some point, I would hope that you love me enough to walk away from what you do, and not make me have to say words over your funeral."

"I'm not gonna do this forever."

"Hopefully you make that decision before it's made for you. I mean, you're still a young guy, but what happens when you're fifty or sixty and your reflexes start slowing down? Are you still going to go out there like you're Chuck Norris or something?"

"Mia, I don't know when it's gonna be. I don't think it's gonna be ten or twenty years from now. I'm closer to the end now than I thought I'd be five years ago. But if you want me to stop today or next month, that's not gonna happen."

"And I don't really expect it to. I just want to know that there's an end in sight. That I'm not going to be made a widow before I'm even married."

Recker wasn't going to promise that he would never be killed out in the street. After what just happened, how could he? All he could do was try to alleviate her fears the best he could.

"I don't know what you want me to say. If you want me to say I'm eventually gonna stop doing this, then yeah, eventually I am. If you want an exact date, that I can't give you."

"Mike," Mia said, shaking her head, trying to choose her words carefully. "At some point, I would like to try for another baby. And I don't want him or her to grow up without a father."

Recker nodded, though there was really nothing else he could say at that point. He just took Mia in his arms and started hugging her.

"We'll figure it out. We always do."

15

Recker and Mia were both getting ready for work. They were sitting down at the table, just about finished their breakfast, when the conversation turned to the situation Recker got out of the day before.

"You never told me about Chris. Is he all right?"

Recker motioned to his face. "Cuts and bruises, just like me."

"Was he shot just like you too?"

Recker faked a smile. "No. I got that special."

"Can I ask what you plan on doing today?"

Recker shrugged. "I dunno. The usual I guess."

"Not with that arm you're not."

"Oh, don't you start too. I already heard this from David yesterday."

"Well he happens to be right. If you go out there trying to use that shoulder, you're going to hurt it more, then you'll really have problems." Mia thought about what she just said, knowing that Recker would really be out of action for a long time if he hurt that shoulder further. The idea actually appealed to her. "You know what, on second thought, go do what you normally do."

"Oh, really?"

"Yes. Hurt it more. Then you'll really have to take a step back."

"For your information, I'm not planning on doing anything physical today."

"Oh," Mia said, a disappointed look on her face.

"I'm just going to the office and working from there. If anything comes up, I'm sure Chris will handle it."

"Speaking of him, what's his face look like?"

"Why don't you call him and see for yourself? Sorry, I didn't think to take pictures."

"Ha ha." Mia did take his advice though and video called Haley. He was still at home as well, getting ready.

"Hey Mia, what's up?"

"Oh god, you look terrible too."

Haley smiled. "Thanks. Good to see you too."

"Mike told me everything that happened yesterday."

"Everything?"

"Everything."

"Oh. How'd that go?"

"About as well as you'd expect," Mia answered.

"Umm, is this my turn to face the music now?"

"Something like that. You gotta be more careful out there!"

"I know, I know. It won't happen again."

"I mean, you guys are supposed to be better than that. Having to be rescued by a mobster and his cronies."

"I promise we'll be better."

"You better, because like I told Mike, I don't wanna be saying words over your funeral either."

"I don't think you'd have to. Who would show up?"

Recker started laughing, drawing a look from Mia that immediately shut him down.

"That's not the point," Mia said. "You know what I mean."

"I know, I know."

"You're like a brother to us, Chris."

"And I love you guys too. It was really all my fault yesterday, anyway. I was the one that got jammed up and made Mike come in after me."

"It doesn't matter. You both need to be more careful."

"We will be. I promise."

After getting off the phone, Recker and Mia cleared the table, then finished getting ready for work. They went to the door and started going their separate ways, giving each other a last second kiss before leaving each other.

"Be careful," Mia said. "Please."

"I promise."

Once Recker got to the office, he was surprised to find it empty. Jones was nowhere to be found. Recker's first inclination was to look for signs of trouble in case someone broke in or there were signs of a struggle, papers thrown around, a mess on the floor, anything like that. There wasn't though. Recker got out his phone and was about to call his friend when the door opened up again. Jones walked in looking safe and sound.

"You all right?"

Noting the concern in his partner's voice, Jones looked a little perplexed. "I'm fine. Why do you ask?"

"Because you're not here."

"What do you mean I'm not here? I'm right here."

"I mean you weren't here when I got here. I don't remember the last time that happened."

"Before you start gloating about you beating me into the office or something, remember I sleep here. I just went out for a walk for a little bit."

"Oh."

"I do do things like that you know from time to time. I don't just sit in this office twenty-four hours a day."

"Good. Exercise is good."

"Thank you, Dr. Spock."

Recker looked confused. "Wasn't he a kids doctor or something?"

Jones walked over to his chair. "Yes, yes, it was just

the name that came to the top of my head first. I realize it doesn't make much sense if you analyze it."

A few minutes later, Haley came walking in.

"Oh good, the gang's all here," Recker said.

"You seem to be in a delightfully good mood for someone who's been shot and whose face looks like it was used as target practice for the local karate dojo."

"He must not have gotten yelled at as much as he thought when he went home," Haley said with a laugh.

"Believe me, I got chewed out plenty."

"And deservedly so," Jones said.

"Yeah, well, let's not get into that again. What's done is done. Let's move on to the next thing."

"Anything on the agenda today?" Haley asked.

"Do you two really think you are able to do anything today in your present condition?" Jones asked.

"I'm sure we can manage."

"Well, one of you might be able to manage. The other one I'm not so sure."

Recker smiled. "Depends on the assignment."

"Yes, well, luckily there are none at the moment. Unless of course we decide to go Scorpion hunting at some point today."

"Not a bad thought."

"A crazy thought for you."

"Wouldn't be the first time, right?"

"Unfortunately so."

A minute later, Jones got a text. "Make sure Mike

doesn't do anything stupid please." Jones smiled upon reading it, drawing a reaction from his partners.

"What's so funny?" Recker asked.

"Oh, nothing."

"You get a daily riddle texted to you or something?" Haley asked.

Jones handed Recker the phone. "She's not funny," Recker said, handing it to his other partner.

"I'd say she's keeping an eye on you even when she can't see you."

"Yeah."

Haley passed the phone back to Jones. "The boss said to keep you in today," Jones said.

Recker could have continued arguing about it, but there wasn't much point. They didn't have a job lined up anyway, so why bother? If push came to shove, he'd go out if he had to. Especially if the Scorpions showed up somewhere.

"Since there's nothing planned for today, guess we're looking for those pointy-tailed devils?" Haley asked.

"That would be the plan," Jones replied.

"What about our regular stuff?" Recker asked. "Anything on the horizon?"

"A few things I'm monitoring. Nothing that seems imminent, though we know how quickly that can change, don't we?"

"Wonder how long before we hear about what Vincent's planning?" Haley asked.

"The real question is going to be whether we're gonna be in on it or whether he lets us know what's going on? Or are we just gonna hear about it after the fact?"

"I have a feeling we will know about that relatively soon," Jones answered.

"More than likely."

"Maybe even before the day is out."

"Well, if I know Vincent, once he makes up his mind, it doesn't take long for him to put his plan into action."

The team worked for the rest of the day, though it wasn't the most strenuous that they ever worked. Without having anything concrete to work on with the Scorpions, and nothing of their own work, they ambled through the day at a pace that they weren't used to. They were used to moving like their hair was on fire. It could have been that two of the three members were still sore and beat up, so they weren't exactly in prime working condition. As they started to wind down the day, though, business was about to pick up. Recker's phone rang, and when he saw it was Malloy calling, instinctively knew something was up. He wasn't calling just to check up on his health.

"How you feeling?" Malloy asked.

"I'm hanging in there."

"Ready to get back in the saddle anytime soon?"

"It would depend on the circumstances. I'm

assuming you're calling with something specific and not just aimless chit-chat."

"Vincent's got a plan to get a lot of the Scorpions in one place. He needs you to make it work though."

"How?"

"He's telling the Scorpions that he's got a meeting with you and he wants them to bring as many of their guys as possible."

"So how's that gonna work?"

"You're gonna be in the middle of some dark creepy warehouse, then when they see you, they're gonna start firing."

"So I'm being used as bait?" Recker asked.

"Something like that."

"Vincent knows you're probably not up for getting down and dirty yourself yet. But you can still lure them in. The only way it'll work is if they think you're there."

"So I'm supposed to let them see me and start shooting?"

"That's the plan. Then when they do that, our guys will come up behind them and mow them down."

"And they won't see them?"

"Our guys will be strategically placed where they're overlooked until the time is right."

"And how many does Vincent plan on taking down in this little... arrangement?"

"He thinks it'll be at least twenty," Malloy answered. "So that's probably about half of what they got left."

"When?"

"Two days from now?"

"And the Scorpions aren't going to get suspicious that they might be getting set up?"

"Vincent's going to tell them some line about how you're starting to infringe on his business and it's time to take you out. He's going to tell them that he's going to meet with you in order to draw you out, then if they want to finish things off, it'll be easy pickings."

"Why not just do a meeting like we did before?" Recker asked.

"Because they wouldn't agree to that again. Not one where they think Haley might take their guys out while they're waiting. That ship's sailed. The only way we'll get a bunch of them out in the open is if they think they can surprise you without you knowing they're there."

It didn't take Recker long to mull it over. Whatever it took to get rid of the Scorpions, he was willing to do. "Count me in."

"I'll call you with specifics tomorrow once we have everything confirmed. Vincent wanted to make sure you were on board before putting things in place."

"OK. I'm not sure how much I'll be able to contribute to this party though."

"All you need to bring is your face. We'll take care of the rest."

Jones and Haley were listening to Recker's conversation and could tell that something was going down.

Once Recker hung up, he told his friends the logistics of the plan so far. As usual, Jones had the most reservations.

"I'm not sure I like that. You're going to let yourself be a target?"

"I'm a target every time I go out there," Recker replied.

"Yes, but this time, you'll actually be using yourself as target practice."

"We've all agreed that I should try to take it easy, right?"

"This doesn't qualify as taking it easy."

"Well, I don't have to do anything, other than show up, then hide when the shooting starts."

"Yes, because we all know how well you hide when the shooting starts."

"It's a chance to take out half of whatever men they got left," Recker said. "I think that's a chance worth taking."

"It's putting your faith into Vincent that he can, and will, protect you."

"Maybe. But I don't see a reason why I shouldn't. Do you?"

"I agree," Haley said. "I think it's a chance we gotta take. Let's bury these crumbs now while we got a chance so we can move on to other things. Besides, I can go too and keep an eye on Mike."

"And what if someone shoots him before you get a chance to keep an eye on him?" Jones asked.

"I've been shot before," Recker answered. "I'll be fine."

"What if it's in the head?"

"Why do you always have to bring up the negative?"

"Because you don't think of it enough. Someone has to."

"Vincent's had chances to take me out long before this if that's what you're thinking."

"That's not really what I'm thinking," Jones said. "My issue is not with trusting Vincent. If that was the case, he wouldn't have bothered to save you yesterday. He's not going to save you one day and turn on you the next. No, my issue is just using yourself as target practice."

"We can all agree that I'm the one that's going to get them to come out in large numbers, right?"

"Probably."

"It's like Chris said, let's bury these guys now so we can finally put them in the rearview mirror."

"I just hope we're not burying you alongside of them."

16

The following morning, Recker and Haley arrived at the office about the same time. They each would have different itineraries for the day though. Jones was monitoring a possible liquor store holdup and was waiting for that last piece of critical information that he needed.

"I would stay loose and ready if I was you," Jones said, looking in Haley's direction as he poured himself some coffee.

"Got something for me?"

"Liquor store. I've got two males, intercepted some text messages, planning to rob the store today. Just waiting on a time."

"What about me?" Recker asked.

"What about you?"

"Got anything for me too?"

"I've got a warm seat beside me if that makes you feel better."

"So maybe I'll just go with Chris then?"

"Or maybe you can just stay here and rest your shoulder like you're supposed to."

"What about these liquor store guys?" Haley asked. "How dangerous are they?"

"Well I believe they will be carrying guns if that answers your question."

"Anyone with a gun is dangerous."

"But they don't appear to be hardened criminals," Jones said. "They're a couple of eighteen, nineteen-year-old kids looking for some money. Minor things in their packages, shoplifting, things like that. Nothing heavy. But I have a feeling you'll have to move quickly when the time comes."

"Why's that?"

"The one asked for a time, so we're just waiting for a reply. I have a feeling when it comes it will be fairly immediate."

"Maybe I should just head down there now and wait," Haley said.

"Might be a good idea..." Jones stopped talking and leaned in closer to his computer, the urgency of whatever it was clearly evident on his face. "Go now! Fifth and Market. You've got thirty minutes to get there."

Haley sped out of the office, flew down the steps and ran to his car, peeling out of the parking lot. Recker got up and watched from the window as his partner went out without him. It wasn't the first time they'd gone out on separate missions, but this time just felt different. Probably because of the wound in Recker's shoulder, it made him feel not as ordinary or maybe as needed as he was used to. Jones saw the expression on his friend's face.

"He'll be fine on his own," Jones said. "It's a couple of teenagers, he can handle them."

"It's not that. I know he doesn't need me on this."

"Then what is it?"

"I just... I feel like the kid in elementary school who's getting punished for something and has to watch all his classmates out on the playground through the classroom window while he writes extra sentences on the blackboard."

Jones laughed. "Not quite the same comparison. You're not being punished."

"I know. It's just what it feels like."

"I wouldn't know."

Recker turned and looked at him. "Why does that not surprise me? You probably never got in trouble while you were in school, did you?"

"Well, not usually."

"Not usually? Admit it, you were a teacher's dream. Always doing what you were supposed to be doing, never goofing off, never talking back, always had your homework done, admit it. You were one of those kids."

"I'll have you know I was not."

"Oh really? What'd you do?"

"I got in trouble plenty of times."

"I don't believe it," Recker said.

"Well it's true."

"Give me an example. Just one."

"What is this? Did you become a therapist and now examining my childhood?"

"I just wanna know what terrible, terrible thing you did in school. C'mon, tell me."

Jones thought for a minute. He had to think long and hard because there really was nothing. Recker was completely right in his assessment of him, not that he liked to admit it.

"You got nothing, do you?" Recker asked.

"No, wait, there is something."

"I'm waiting."

"OK, well, yeah, there was this time when..."

"Yeah?"

"Ummm..."

"David, just admit it, you were a perfect child."

"I was not. I got into plenty of incidents, believe me."

"So tell me one."

"Well, they're not all coming to me at the moment."

Recker shook his head, not believing him at all. "You didn't have a single problem, did you?"

"I did. It's just... with Chris being out there, my mind and focus is on him and it's tough to concentrate on anything else."

"Oh, OK. Maybe later when he's done, you'll think of something."

Haley raced to the liquor store, not sure if he was going to get there on time or not. It was going to be close. It really depended on traffic, which was always anyone's guess when traveling on I-95. He hoped he could get there before the kids had a chance to do something stupid that they'd regret for the rest of their lives. Once they pulled this job, there was no turning back. Haley also hoped he could prevent this robbery without violence. They were a couple of young kids who probably needed more guidance in their lives. He'd hate to have to kill them if they came up shooting. He was hopeful that he would be able to stop the robbery peacefully, but that was up to them more than it would be him. Haley always hoped not to have to use his gun. It just sometimes, maybe more often than not, didn't turn out that way.

By the time Haley got to the liquor store, he peeked in the front window and saw the two kids already in the store by the counter. They each had a gun out and pointed at the cashier, who was also the owner of the place. Haley sighed, frustrated that he didn't get there in time, and also that they had guns. A person usually didn't carry a gun unless he intended to use it. He could only assume that was the case here.

Haley quickly thought of his options, but there were only three that crossed his mind. He could go around to the back and hope a door was open, that way he could try to catch them by surprise. But they could've been gone by the time he got back there. Or the door might have been locked, wasting valuable time. He could go right through the front door, guns out, firing away, hitting everything in sight. Or, he could pretend he was a regular customer and walk through the door, pretending he didn't know there was a robbery in progress.

Aiming for as little violence as possible, Haley chose the third option. He was going to try to give the kids every possible chance to walk away from this without holes in their bodies. If he went in guns blazing, he knew he could kill them both, but that wasn't what he was looking for. Considering neither of them were hardened criminals, Haley wanted to give them a chance to put themselves on the right path. The rest was up to them.

Haley kept his gun tight inside his belt, where it was easily reachable if he needed to use it. He opened the door, whistling as he walked through it. He pretended like he didn't even see the robbers there yet. Once the bell went off over the door, signaling a customer, both kids turned and pointed their guns at Haley.

"Hey, just stop right there, man!"

"What's going on?" Haley asked, paying close attention to their weapons.

"What do you think's going on?"

"Looks like you guys are making a bad life choice."

"What?!"

"I said, you guys really oughtta think about what you're doing."

"Are you crazy? Man, I should shoot you right now," the kid said, pointing his gun right at Haley's face.

"I don't think that would be very smart. Listen, I'm giving you a chance now. Just go on, go home, forget this ever happened and go find yourselves a couple of jobs and live the right way, huh?"

The kids looked at each other, thinking the guy was some kind of kook. "Man, you're crazy."

Haley sighed, realizing the kids were hardheaded and stubborn and that he'd have to do things the hard way. He reached for his gun, pulling it out and aiming at both kids, pointing it at both of them equally.

"Which one of you wants the first one?"

Both kids immediately dropped their guns on the ground and threw their hands up. "Yo, man, it wasn't even loaded. I swear!"

"Please don't shoot," the second kid said.

"Listen, what do you guys wanna go around doing things like this for?" Haley asked.

"People gotta eat."

"So get a job."

"Where? Some fast-food joint or something?"

"So? Nothing wrong with that. It's a steady job, making money, and best of all, you don't have to worry about getting shot or going to jail, both of which could happen here, and will happen for sure if you try something like this again. As long as you're working, there's no shame in anything that you do."

The kids looked at each other, Haley's words possibly getting through to them. They really weren't bad kids. The guns they were carrying weren't even real. They were fakes, but Haley recognized that as soon as he looked at them. They looked real to the untrained eye, but he could tell right off that they weren't the genuine thing. He knew the kids weren't really looking to hurt anybody. They were just young and dumb, looking to make a little money.

"So what do you wanna do about these guys?" Haley asked.

"Me?" the owner asked. "Aren't you the cop?"

Haley shook his head. "I'm not a cop."

"You're not?"

"You're not?!" the kids said in unison. "Who the hell are you then?" the first kid asked.

"Uh, you can call me one of the Silencers."

"One of?! You're one of the Silencers?!"

"That's right."

"Man, how many of you guys are out there?!"

"Uh, just two."

"Man, this is off the hook."

Haley looked to the owner again. "So you wanna call the cops, tell them you got a couple of kids trying to rob you, or you wanna let them go?"

The owner looked at the kids, who had fearful

expressions on their faces, and sighed, not believing what he was about to do. "Let them go. As long as they promise never to come in here again."

"Oh, we promise, mister! Never again!"

"OK, you can go," Haley said. "But remember this before you leave. I know your names. I'm gonna be watching for you. And if you try something like this again, I'm gonna be there, and the next time you won't be so lucky. You only get one second chance."

"Don't worry, mister, we won't try something like this again."

"I hope not." Haley reached into his pocket and removed some money. He handed one of the kids a ten-dollar bill. "Here. Why don't you kids find a fast-food joint and have yourselves some lunch? Then when you're done, apply for a job." The kids nodded. "Now go on, get out of here."

The kids raced out of the store, thankful to get a second chance. Once they were gone, Haley went over to their guns and picked them up.

"That was a nice thing you did there," the owner said.

"Me? You're the one that could've called the cops on them."

"Yeah, well, I dunno, just seemed like the right thing to do. Hopefully, your little message sinks in on them."

"Yeah, me too. I don't think they were bad kids."

Haley held up one of their guns and pointed it at

the window. The owner looked confused at what he was doing. Haley pulled the trigger on the gun. Nothing happened.

"It wasn't loaded?" the owner asked.

"Not even real."

"What?"

"Fakes. Both of them."

"Well I'll be. I didn't even notice. Looked real enough to me."

"It would to most people," Haley said.

"You knew that as soon as you came in the door, didn't you?"

Haley nodded. "Yeah."

"That's why you were talking to them like that."

"You don't think I'd be taking chances and talking so much with guys that had loaded guns do you?"

The owner smiled and shook his head. "That's something else. Hey, you mind if I spread the word around that you were in here?"

"I guess not."

"I appreciate that. I got robbed a few months back, and then this here today, if word spreads around that the Silencers are watching the store, that's as good as having a neon sign out front that says stay away."

"Go right ahead."

"Might also help to get some publicity and get some more customers in here if they know the Silencers are around," the man said with a laugh.

"Whatever helps you out."

"Thanks. Did you really mean what you said about knowing their names and keeping an eye out for them. Or was that just talk to get them to listen?"

"I really meant it."

"How could you know who they are though if you never met them before?"

Haley, though knowing the man was well-intentioned, had no interest in discussing their methods. He walked over to the door and looked back at him before leaving.

"We have our ways."

17

It was later in the afternoon, a full day since Haley's incident at the liquor store. They were all sitting at their desks working, wondering why the Scorpions had become so silent. They were also wondering when they were going to get the call about Vincent's meeting.

"It could be they're licking their wounds," Jones said. "They might just be admitting defeat for now and not planning on doing anything until they get strength back in their numbers."

Recker wasn't so sure though. It certainly made sense on some level. He wasn't sure the Scorpions operated like that though. "I dunno. I don't think they're capable of admitting defeat. I think it goes against everything they stand for. They pride them-selves in being tougher, meaner, and badder than everyone else. Going somewhere to hide for six months while they go on a recruiting spree... I don't know if they're capable of that."

"I don't think they are," Haley said. "Maybe they're just quiet because they're planning something. They haven't left. And they won't unless it's in a box."

A few minutes later, Recker's phone rang. It was the call they'd been waiting for.

"Yeah?"

"It's all set," Malloy said. "Tomorrow at noon. Vincent wants to meet you at eleven though so he can go over everything with you. He knows how much you hate being in the dark."

"I'd appreciate that."

"Where?"

"Usual spot. The warehouse where we've been having the meetings at."

"I thought it was going to be somewhere new?"

"Vincent thinks this is better. It'll be easier to get our boys into position without having to move them to a new building. It'll work."

"Scorpions are coming?" Recker asked.

"That's what they say."

"How many?"

"Don't know for sure. Vincent didn't want to press and get specific numbers thinking they might think something was up. He just said he could get you into a position they could take you out if they brought enough men to get the job done."

"That could be anything from three to twenty."

"I know. Like I said, though, he didn't want to press. Knowing how many men they've lost to this point, and how badly they probably wanna kill you, I'd be highly surprised if it was anything less than ten."

"Yeah, well, let's hope they bring everyone and the kitchen sink," Recker said. "I wanna get this over with."

"You and me both, brother. We'll get it done though."

"What about Chris?"

"Have him come at eleven too. We already got a spot picked out for him."

"Is it overlooking my position?"

Recker could hear Malloy smiling through the phone. "I already figured that's the way you wanted it. I assumed you wanted him watching your back more than anyone so I got him in position to see you at all times. Unless you scatter somewhere, then you're on your own."

"Works for me."

"All right, see you then."

Once Recker got off the phone, he relayed the plan to the others. "Looks like we're all set for noon tomorrow. Me and Chris get there at eleven so Vincent can give us the plan."

"I still don't like going into this blind," Jones said.

"We're not. That's why we're meeting Vincent at eleven. So he gives us the scoop."

"Yeah, an hour ahead of time. What if his vision of things doesn't match up with yours?"

"I think Vincent knows what he's doing. He didn't get to where he's at by planning like an idiot."

"That's clearly not what I said. But the way he does things, and the way we do things, don't always align properly."

"It'll be fine," Recker said, nodding confidently. "It'll be fine."

"And we don't even know how many of the Scorpions will be there. It might only be two of them. Then what good would that do? Vincent will be outed over nothing."

"Oh my gosh, David, why do you always have to be a Debbie Downer?"

"I've already explained this to you before. It's because you don't look at the bad side of things enough."

"I look at them, I look at them. I just shrug them off and proceed, anyway."

"I'm fully aware."

"I don't think Vincent would proceed with this thing, and give up being neutral in all this, unless he was positively sure we were going to get at least half of what's left. I mean, do you really think he'd do this if he thought they were only bringing two?"

"Probably not," Jones answered. "But what if he's wrong? It has been known to happen you know."

Recker threw his hands up in the air and leaned back in his chair, covering his eyes with his arms.

"Here, you talk to him," he said, pointing at his other partner.

"Closing your eyes and pretending there's no issue doesn't make the problem go away."

"The only problem here is you."

"Guys, guys," Haley said, finally interjecting to stop the argument from getting out of hand. "There's a simple way to handle all this to everyone's satisfaction."

"And what's that?" Jones asked.

"We go meet Vincent at eleven tomorrow as planned. Once he tells us his plan, if we like it, we stick with it. If we don't, we walk away. Or, we suggest a different one and see what he says. That way, it's no harm, no foul."

"See?" Recker said. "The voice of reason."

Jones briefly looked at the two of them. "I suppose that might work."

"And if we decide to walk away," Haley said. "Then Vincent still has time to call the whole thing off and doesn't give himself up in the process. He can simply say we had something else come up and couldn't attend. This way everyone wins."

"Does that work for you?" Recker asked.

"I already said that would suffice," Jones said, a slight irritation in his voice.

"Oh, well, as long as it suffices."

"Mockery will not win you any friends."

"Since when did I try to win any?"

"Why do I get the feeling this is going to be a long night?"

"Because you're probably gonna talk all day about what might go wrong."

Jones blinked and shook his head. "A very long night."

The following morning, the team met up at the office again at nine o'clock. Recker and Haley wanted to make sure there was nothing pressing coming up in Jones' computer that they had to take care of first. Even though Jones told them before they came in that it wasn't necessary, it had become kind of a ritual at this point. It would have felt weird not going into the office first, then going back out. It was just what they were used to now. And while nobody on the team was overly superstitious, they did like sticking to as much of the same routine as possible. It helped to normalize things in a job that didn't have much normalcy in it.

"Any last-minute objections?" Recker said, closing his gun cabinet.

"No," Jones replied. "I believe we said all that yesterday."

"Just thought I'd check."

"If the plan isn't to our liking, we will walk away, correct?"

"Will do."

Jones then pointed at Haley. "I'm counting on you being the voice of reason here. Don't let him snow you into staying if you don't feel comfortable with what's going on. Walk away if you feel it's the right thing to do."

"Don't worry," Haley said. "If the plan's no good, I'll throw him over my shoulder and scoot out of there."

Recker laughed, imagining the scenario in his mind. "Let's try to make this quick though, huh? Got plans later."

"You... have plans?" Jones asked. "Anything you would like to share with the rest of us?"

"It's not work related. It's personal. Mia's off today..."

Jones put his hand up to prevent hearing any more personal details. "Say no more. We don't need to know what's planned."

Recker rolled his eyes. "Get your mind out of the gutter. Mia's off today, and she wanted me to take it easy..."

"So you're listening to that by making yourself a target and getting into a firefight with a bunch of deadly men in a warehouse owned by a mobster. Makes perfect sense."

"Will you let me finish?"

"Proceed."

"Mia's off today."

"We got that part."

"You're not gonna let me finish, are you?"

"OK, I'm done."

"Mia is off today," Recker said, somewhat sternly this time, hoping he wouldn't get interrupted again. "So she wanted me to come home early and take it easy. So, since there's not much going on, and everyone here wanted me to take it easy, I said I would only put in half a day at the office, then go home. Is that OK?"

Jones scratched his ear. "Well... I love how you say you are going to take it easy, like this whole warehouse thing is some kind of afterthought. Like it's no big deal."

"It's not."

"I don't know, Mike, someday you might have to live in the same world as the rest of us and actually understand what danger is."

"I'm a trained black ops CIA agent. We don't understand danger like normal people. We embrace it, thrive upon it, live with it. It's just another day."

Jones pointed at their partner. "Then why is he not quite as... danger-seeking?"

Recker looked at Haley and shrugged. "I put in more time than him?"

"So you're more brainwashed?"

"I'm not brainwashed. I just think differently than most."

Jones chuckled. "Well I'll certainly agree with that."

"And I don't seek danger. I just don't run from it either."

It was ten-thirty, and Recker and Haley finished getting ready to leave. They bid their partner and team founder goodbye as they walked out the door for their rendezvous with Vincent.

Jones stared at the door for a few moments after they left. "You don't run from danger. Even when you should."

18

Recker and Haley drove over to the warehouse together, getting there only a few minutes before eleven o'clock. Once they drove through the gate, they immediately saw Malloy standing in the parking lot, waiting for them. They got out of the car, greeted Malloy by shaking hands, then were led inside to meet up with Vincent. There was no time to waste with idle chit-chat. Malloy led the pair into a different part of the building that Recker had never been in before. He'd only even been in the office area up to that point. They found Vincent standing in the middle of the room, apparently sizing up the room, watching a few of his men work by moving boxes around. He noticed his guests approaching and smiled at them.

"Mike, Chris, glad you could make it."

"Nice setup you got here," Recker said, observing a

half-filled warehouse. "There something actually in those boxes?"

Vincent grinned, though he wouldn't answer the questions. "I will neither confirm nor deny there is anything in those boxes."

In reality, it was one of the places where Vincent kept some of the various merchandise, like guns, jewelry, paintings, counterfeit money, along with other items that were waiting to be sold, most of which was acquired through illegal means.

"And I'll take your word that you'll forget everything you see in here after you leave."

"You got it," Recker said.

"That's good enough for me." Vincent then looked at Haley. "Same goes for you."

"I can't even remember how to get here," Haley replied.

Vincent smiled. "So, on to our business here today. I'm assuming you wanna know what I've got cooking?"

"It would be nice to... have an idea of what's going on," Recker said.

"So here's the deal. I told the Scorpions I was bringing you here under the disguise of making some kind of truce between you. Then I told them to bring as many boys as they could, because we were gonna bury you here. I made up some story about you pissing me off and getting in the way of some of my deals and that's why I wanted you rubbed off."

"Hope it doesn't turn out to be true. The burying me here part."

"Relax, it'll be fine. Anyway, you're gonna leave after we're done talking here and come back at twelve. Chris can stay here. When you come back, you'll be led in here, where I'll be standing against that wall over there. Naylor should be here already. Then the three of us are gonna start talking. I'm supposed to give a line to indicate when his boys are supposed to start shooting. I'm obviously never gonna say that line."

"What is it?"

"It's supposed to be, I'm not gonna take that from a punk like you."

"OK."

"Instead, my boys are listening for a different line. When I say, I'm sorry things had to turn out this way, they're gonna take out whatever Scorpions they see."

"I need Chris in a spot he can see me."

"Already arranged. Second floor up there," Vincent said, pointing to it. "He'll have a perfect vantage spot to see where you are."

"Where are the Scorpions going to be?"

Vincent pointed to the far wall. "They'll be behind those boxes and crates over there. They'll already be there and hiding when you come in."

"And your boys?"

"I'll have a few down here on both sides of them, so they can cut them down in the crossfire and they have nowhere to escape." Vincent pointed to the second-floor balcony again. "I'll also have a few boys up top shooting down."

"And you don't think they have any idea this is a setup?"

"Shouldn't. And they won't see my boys waiting for them either. Everything will proceed like it normally would with any other meeting. Once you arrive, my boys will get into position."

"Have you given any thought to them shooting you first before you give that line, then shooting me?"

Vincent smiled, appreciating Recker's thinking. "I have. It's not a concern. I have that taken care of."

Recker wasn't sure how he could have that taken care of, but figured it was better not to ask. Of course, it was likely that Vincent wouldn't tell him, anyway. As long as he had already thought of the potential, and was prepared for it, the rest was on him.

"Do you have any idea how many men they're bringing?" Recker asked.

"I am expecting around a dozen. No less than ten for sure, maybe as many as fifteen. Any other questions?"

"Yeah. When the shooting starts, we're going to be exposed just standing there. It's a long way to get to some cover."

"Where we'll be standing," Vincent said, pointing to the spot. "The wall cuts back a little, we can go just beyond the corner and we should be fine."

"And Naylor?"

"He should be one of the first ones to go."

Recker nodded, feeling like the plan was solid. Not perfect, but solid. He turned to his partner to get his feelings. "What do you think?"

"Sounds like a plan to me," Haley answered.

"All right. Let's do this."

"OK. Chris, go with Jimmy," Vincent said. "He'll take you to your spot on the second floor." Vincent then pointed at Recker. "You can come back at twelve."

"Should I be fashionably late or should I come early?"

Vincent smiled. "You can come right on time."

Recker gave Haley a wave as he walked away. Recker went back to his car and drove off for a little bit, sitting on a side street, still having the front of the warehouse in his view. He wanted to see for himself how many Scorpions were showing up before he arrived. Though he trusted Vincent, Recker still liked having as many details as possible. And he wasn't fond of going in there without knowing how many men they were up against. And while he probably wasn't going to be able to see exactly how many men were in each car, he figured he could get a pretty good idea by seeing the amount of cars that arrived.

While Recker was outside, Malloy was showing Haley the spot he could take up that would give him a good vantage point of Recker's position. He took him to a spot in the corner, on the side Recker would be.

Haley would basically be looking down right on top of his partner.

"This is as good a spot as any," Malloy said.

"Yeah, it'll work. Where are you gonna be?"

"I'll be down below. You got eyes on Recker. I got eyes on Vincent."

Haley laughed. "We might be shooting at the same target."

"Could be."

"How's Recker gonna be moving down there if it gets hot? His shoulder OK?"

"Well he's not gonna be doing any cartwheels or flips or anything, but he should be OK. He's still got a good arm to shoot with and that's all he needs."

"I just wanna make sure he's not a lame duck out there," Malloy said.

"He'll be alright. And if not... that's what I'm here for."

Malloy nodded. "Hopefully we tie this thing off today. I'm already tired of dealing with these people."

"How many men you got set up?"

Malloy looked around and then started pointing throughout the warehouse. "Well, we got two, four, six, eight, ten, twelve people up top here. They'll just be shooting down at the Scorpions position. They'll be out of sight when they get here. Then down there we'll have two, four, about ten more down there, so about twenty-two altogether. Not including you, me, and Recker."

"That gives us about twenty-five. Should be enough to get the job done."

"And that's assuming they bring everyone. They might not. It should be enough no matter what."

Everyone inside the building used the rest of the time to go over last-minute details and get themselves ready. There was an anticipation throughout the room, it could be felt without anyone really saying anything. It just felt like this was going to be the last anyone heard from the Scorpions. Once Malloy left Haley to his own devices and checked on the rest of the men, Haley checked in with Recker to see where he was.

"How you making out?"

"Good," Recker answered. "Just sitting down the street, keeping an eye on the building."

"See anything yet?"

"No, it's pretty quiet so far. They still got a little time to go. How's it looking in there?"

"Good," Haley replied. "I think they got everything under control."

"Let's just hope the Scorpions bring enough men so this isn't all for nothing."

"I've been thinking, they might bring everyone they got. I mean, think about it. Vincent told them to bring enough men to take you out. But they've also got him standing there in front of them. That's a heck of an enticement, don't you think?"

"Yeah, I do."

"I mean, could they really pass up the opportunity

to take out both you and him at the same time? That would be like a dream come true for them, wouldn't it? Then they wouldn't have to worry about either of you later."

"That's probably what Vincent was thinking too."

After they got done talking, Recker called Jones, just to let him know that the plan was satisfactory and they were staying. He didn't want Jones to be left in the dark as to what they were doing.

"You're staying, aren't you?" Jones asked before Recker was able to get a word out.

"Chris already call you?"

"He didn't have to. I knew no matter what that you two were going to stay. Even if you didn't like Vincent's plan, you would come up with something that allowed you to stay and finish things off. I know you too well. I knew you wouldn't just walk away from something like this."

"Well, as it turns out, we didn't have to think of anything else. I think Vincent's got it under control."

"We'll see about that after the shooting stops."

"Chris is gonna have a spot almost right on top of me. Everything's gonna be fine."

"And do you know yet how many Scorpions are going to be there?"

"Not yet. Vincent thinks at least a dozen. We'll see. Doesn't really matter though. While I'd like for it to be all of them, even if it's not, any opportunity we have to keep dwindling their numbers is a good thing."

"Yes, I suppose so."

"No need to worry. This'll go off without a hitch and we'll be back before you know it."

Jones raised his eyebrows at the comment. He knew things rarely went without a hitch or an issue. "Because that happens so often, right?"

"It'll work, David. It'll work. Trust me."

19

R ecker perked up in his seat a little when he saw several cars in a row turn into the warehouse building. There were four cars waiting to be let in by Vincent's guard at the gate. Recker tried looking through the windows of some of the cars, but they were tinted, so he couldn't get a good look at the amount of men inside. If each vehicle had four people inside, that meant they brought sixteen with them. At minimum they brought eight. Either way, Recker figured it was a healthy amount of bodies to take down.

After a minute of waiting, the gate was opened, and the Scorpions were allowed to drive through. Recker lost sight of them as they drove up to the building, walls and trees getting in his way. He looked at the time. He still had fifteen minutes until he was supposed to appear. He wanted to just go in now and get it over with, but he had to be patient and stick to the plan, especially since it wasn't his and he wasn't the main player in this charade.

Once the Scorpions made their way inside the building, they were immediately greeted by Malloy, who then brought the leader over to see Vincent, who was already standing in his spot. The rest of the Scorpions remained near the door. Vincent looked a little confused as the man was brought to him considering it was not who he expected. Vincent looked at the bunch of Scorpions standing around, not seeing Naylor's face among them.

"Mr. Vincent?" the Scorpion said.

"And who might you be?"

"They call me Butch."

Vincent looked the man over. He was a big man, in his mid-thirties, standing about six foot-three, and hovering close to two-hundred and fifty pounds. He had long shaggy hair and a goatee. He was the prototype look for how the gang wanted to appear. "How fitting and appropriate."

"I'm in charge of the group today."

"And where is Mr. Naylor? I was under the impression I would be dealing with him."

"He had kind of a tickle in his throat and thought he should stay in bed and take care of that," Butch said with a smile.

Vincent did not crack one though, not finding it

amusing. "I like for the people I do business with to stick with the plan that they agree to."

Butch shrugged, not really caring. They were there, and that's all that mattered to them. "When's the hotshot getting here?"

"If you're referring to Mr. Recker, he should be here at twelve as I requested him to." Vincent then looked at the men again. "How many men did you bring with you?"

"Fourteen including myself. It should be enough to get the job done. I mean, after all, it's only one guy, right?"

"Unless he brings his partner, which I'm not sure of yet. We'll know more when Recker gets here."

"Fine. Where you want us to set up?"

"You wait here with me," Vincent answered. "Jimmy will show your men where I want them."

"Good deal. One man, two, don't matter, he can bring a whole army with him if he wants to. We'll take care of it."

"I certainly hope so. I'm putting my neck on the line here."

"Naylor wanted me to tell you he appreciated you setting this up. He's planning on giving you some type of gift after it's over."

"I can hardly wait."

Malloy showed the rest of the Scorpions where to go, lining them up behind a bunch of crates and boxes along the far wall. They were sufficiently hidden for the time being. Once he was done getting them situated, he reported back to his boss.

"Anything else?"

"No thank you, Jimmy," Vincent replied. "You can go out to the gate and wait for our other guest."

Malloy nodded, then walked outside. He wasn't technically supposed to wait for Recker, as he was supposed to go outside, then come back in through a side door, then go up to the second floor via another entrance that the Scorpions wouldn't be able to see. But since he was out there, he figured he'd wait for Recker, anyway. As they were waiting for Recker to arrive, Haley looked down from his perch, sizing up the room. He didn't quite like where Recker would be coming in at. It wasn't too far away from where the Scorpions were, and if they didn't stick to the script and wait for Vincent's cue, they could've just opened fire and kill him long before he ever got to Vincent and Butch.

"Hey Mike, you go through the gate yet?"

Recker hadn't yet moved from his spot. "Not yet, why? What's up?"

"The Scorpions are lined up behind some crates near the door where you'd be coming in. That's making me nervous."

"Why?"

"Well, if they decide to open up before Vincent gives his signal, you'll be dead as a doornail long before you get to him. And if they plan on killing

Vincent too, they might not be listening to him, anyway."

"Good point."

"Maybe come in a different direction. Malloy went outside, not sure if he's still out there or not."

"I'll go through the gate now and see."

Recker immediately drove down the street and turned into the property, Vincent's man waving him through the gate. As Recker pulled up to the warehouse, he saw Malloy milling around. He got out of the car and went over to him.

"Everything's in place," Malloy said. "Just waiting for you."

"I figured you'd be in your spot already."

"Supposed to be. Figured I'd wait for you to get here. Give me a few minutes to get up there, huh?"

"Sure. Is there another way in besides that way?" Recker asked, pointing at the door he was supposed to enter.

"Yeah, why?"

"Chris thinks it might not be a good idea for me to go in that way."

"Why not?"

"What happens if the Scorpions decide not to wait for their cue and start blasting at me when I walk in?"

Malloy thought about it for a second. "Yeah. Good point."

"So what other way can I go in?"

Malloy started walking and waved for Recker to follow. "C'mon. We'll go this way."

Recker followed him, walking around the corner of the warehouse to another door. This one led to the office area, one that Recker had never been in before. Malloy unlocked the door so the two men could go inside. They went down a long hallway, then turned left. They then came to another door. It was a brown wooden door with no glass, so Recker couldn't see what was on the other side of it.

"This leads out to the warehouse," Malloy said.

"Good. How much time do you need to get into position?"

"Not enough. I'll just wing it from down here."

"You sure?"

"Yeah. There's another door on the other side of the warehouse. I can come in through there, that way I can keep an eye on you guys from the ground. Haley's got up top covered. Just give me two minutes to get to that side."

"They gonna spot you coming in?" Recker asked.

"Shouldn't. I'll come in real quiet. There's enough stuff over there that I can stay out of sight."

"You'll be able to cover us from there?"

"Should be able to. If not, I'll move closer. Just give me two minutes."

Recker nodded. "You got it."

Malloy scurried off, quickly moving out of sight. Recker looked at his watch so he knew when the two minutes were up. While he was waiting, he figured he'd let Haley know where he was coming in, as best he could tell, anyway.

"Chris, I'm in the building. Malloy let me in a side door."

Haley peeked over the railing, trying to locate the other doors. "Which one?"

"I don't know. Should be east of the door I was supposed to come in at. It's a big brown wooden door. At least from my side it is."

"Hold on, let me see if I can get a better look here."

"Should put me closer to where Vincent is I think."

Haley continued looking around some boxes, though he was careful not to stick his head out too far and have someone down below recognize him. He moved a couple things in front of him to the side to give him a better view.

"Uh, I see a brown door to the right of Vincent, maybe about twenty feet over. That's gotta be it."

"Yeah, must be," Recker said. "You see another door on the other side? Malloy said he's gonna come through that and stay down here."

Haley quickly looked across to the other side of the warehouse, only seeing the bottom half of the other door. The rest of it was obscured by his vantage point and the bottom of the second floor.

"Yeah, I see something. Can't see all of it from here."

"OK."

"When you coming in?"

"One more minute," Recker answered. "Just giving Malloy enough time to sneak in. Let me know if you see him come through."

Haley kept his eyes glued to the other door, waiting to see the bottom half of it open. About thirty seconds later, he did, seeing the shoes and lower legs of a man walking through.

"All right, he's in. Looks like the party's just waiting for you now."

"Looks like I forgot the cake," Recker joked.

"Don't worry about it," Haley laughed. "We brought the gifts that'll keep on giving."

20

"Here goes nothing," Recker said, putting his hand on the handle of the door.

He opened it up and stepped through. Vincent had his hands in his pockets and turned to see who was coming in, surprised that it was Recker. He knew there must have been a reason he deviated from the plan. And he knew someone must have let him in that way, so he continued to play it cool. Recker approached Vincent and the Scorpion, sizing up the big man. Recker of course knew who Butch was from all the advance scouting that they did on the group. He and Butch locked eyes and stared at each other as Recker joined the two men standing there waiting for him.

"Who's this guy?" Recker asked.

"This is Butch," Vincent answered. "He is taking Mr. Naylor's place today."

"I don't negotiate with the second team."

"Who you calling second team?" Butch asked.

"You don't look like you could lead the Girl Scouts."

"You know what your problem is?"

"We don't have time to go down the list," Recker replied.

"Your problem is you don't know when to shut that big mouth of yours."

"You gonna shut it for me?"

"Maybe."

"Good luck. Can we get on with this, I got things to do."

Vincent looked to Butch one more time before he was about to give the order.

"We're gonna give you one last chance," Butch said. "One more chance to save yourself."

"From what?"

"Us. I'm giving you one more opportunity. I suggest you take it. Walk out of here now, leave town, go to some other city, and we won't kill you."

"Because you've been doing so well lately, I guess I should consider that some kind of honor that you're asking so nicely?"

Butch grinned. "You know, I'm really glad you're not taking the offer. That would deprive me the joy out of doing this."

Butch wasn't waiting for any signal from Vincent. The orders they got from Naylor was to kill Recker first, then Vincent. They considered it a bonus to take

Vincent out too, then they could take over the city with relatively little problems from there on out. They didn't expect to have much difficulty with the rest of Vincent's men after he was taken out of the picture. And they weren't sure they would ever get a better opportunity than this, when they were basically invited to kill the both of them. Butch reached into his jacket and removed a pistol. He immediately pointed it at the more dangerous of the two, at least as far as killing him at that moment. And that would be Recker.

Surprised by the suddenness of the action, Recker didn't have time to reach for his own gun, though he did start to make the effort. He didn't have to though. Just as Butch put the gun in the air and aimed at Recker's head, blood exploded out of his chest, the force of the bullet entering his body and knocking the big man off his feet. Recker instantly turned around and looked up at the second floor, seeing Haley standing there with a rifle resting on his shoulder.

Gunfire then erupted all over the warehouse, the bullets flying fast and furious. Recker immediately grabbed Vincent by the arm and pulled him over to the corner of the room, where Vincent instructed him to go before. They reached it safely, nestling themselves in between the wall and some crates until the action died down. And hopefully the Scorpions with it. While they were watching the activity unfold, the rest of the warehouse sounded like a war zone. The noise was amplified in a small enclosed space. Assault rifles, pistols, shotguns, they were all being fired in a wild and intense conflict. Bullets rained down on the Scorpions in all directions. From both sides, from above, there was little chance of them escaping. Their only chance was to kill everyone in their wake. But that was an unlikely task. One by one, the Scorpions started dropping.

Haley looked on at the carnage from his perch on the second floor. He didn't partake in the assault. It didn't seem like it was necessary. Vincent had enough men there to get the job done. It almost didn't seem fair, Haley thought. He quickly rectified those thoughts remembering who was on the other end of the onslaught. Haley turned his attention back to Recker's position, not that he could see him at the moment. But if any of the Scorpions left their position and was able to somehow break through and go after his partner, Haley would make sure he stopped them before they reached their destination.

Though the Scorpions fought back the best they could, and defended themselves well, they really didn't have a chance. Four of them were killed immediately when Vincent's men fired on them, catching them off-guard. The rest were just in survival mode from there on out. And that didn't go very well. Over the next few minutes, their numbers continued dwindling, until there was only one left. He put up a valiant fight, but it was short-lived. A bullet entered his head, finally ending the conflict. The guns stopped firing, causing the room to go eerily silent.

Everyone came out from their positions to survey the damage. Malloy went over to Recker and Vincent to make sure they were OK. Once he saw they were, he went over to the Scorpions location and checked to see if they were all dead. While they were doing that, Haley, along with the other men that were up there, descended down to the first floor. He immediately found his partner. They nodded at each other upon seeing the other.

"Good shooting," Recker said.

Vincent nodded, agreeing. "Yes, quick on the trigger. It was a good thing you were paying attention up there."

"Well, I figured they might not have been on the same track as you and wait for your signal."

"He was probably going to blow both of us away," Recker said, letting Vincent know how close he came to being a memory.

"I guess I'll owe you another one."

Recker shook his head, not interested in IOU's at the present. They'd both done enough for each other where it didn't seem like it mattered anymore. "I think we both did things for each other here."

A few minutes later, Malloy came over to the threesome.

"What's the score?" Vincent asked.

"They're all dead."

"Excellent."

"I guess this all went pretty well," Malloy said.

"As good as could be expected, wouldn't you say?" Vincent asked, looking at Recker.

Recker nodded, thinking there wasn't much he could really add. "Yeah, I'd say so."

"A little hiccup in the beginning, but the end result is what counts."

"That's all that matters."

"How you gonna clean all this up?" Haley asked.

Vincent grinned. "We'll take care of it. That's right, you gentlemen usually don't remain for the aftermaths of your battles. We usually have a little more experience in clean-up, putting everything back together so it looks the way it did previously so no one ever thinks anything happened here."

"Need us to help with anything?" Recker asked.

Vincent put his hand up, appreciating the offer. "No, thank you, Mike. We'll handle it just fine."

"Where are these guys gonna end up?" Haley asked. "Too many for the river, aren't there?"

"I would say so. I'm thinking they might get taken out to the suburbs somewhere, find a nice open, empty field, then buried together. Or maybe we'll just start a big bonfire, burn them to a crisp so they're never identified."

"Takes cremating to a whole 'nother level," Recker said.

"Regardless of where they end up," Vincent said. "They'll be somewhere that's appropriate for them."

Recker and Haley finished talking to Vincent, then left the building and the carnage behind them. They drove back to the office, letting Jones know they were fine, and the details of what happened, that way he wasn't so anxious before they got back and could breathe a sigh of relief. By the time they got back to the office, Jones seemed calmer than usual. He didn't seem as uptight as he usually was, maybe because there was actually an end in sight to the Scorpion problem. What seemed like a daunting task to begin with, with the Scorpions having over eighty members, now seemed like nothing more than a nuisance, with their numbers dwindling down to no more than a handful, or ten at best. They all seemed upbeat, happy with the outcome at Vincent's warehouse, though they still realized there was a threat out there.

"This thing still won't be over until we get Naylor," Recker said.

"I've been seeing what I can do to track him down while you were on the way over here," Jones said. "Phone records, credit cards, that sort of thing, but he doesn't appear to have used anything that I can trace him with. At least not yet."

"And he probably won't. He'll probably stick with cash, aliases, and disguises. He knows he's on borrowed time."

"Well that's the thing. Does he know he's in real

trouble and is just going to escape to somewhere else? Or is he going to double down and try to fight back?"

"If there's one thing we know about the Scorpions... it's that they don't run. They'll stand and fight to the end. No matter what the odds, no matter what the cost, they will return. He's not going anywhere."

"I guess that begs the question of when he will show his face again? Will he do so quickly? Or will he wait until he assembles an army again?"

Recker didn't have an answer. At least not one he could be sure of. He hoped Naylor would show his face again soon. But they couldn't count on that. It was entirely possible that the man wouldn't pop up again for eight months, when he had another legion of men behind him. Whenever he did show his face again, they would have to be ready.

21

Two weeks went by, and all was quiet on the Scorpion front. Recker used that time wisely and took it easy, letting his shoulder heal. He was almost back to a full range of motion, though he still felt a twinge in it every now and then in certain spots. It seemed as if everything was getting back to normal. Haley took most of the assignments for the previous couple of weeks, letting Recker ease his way back into it. Recker did take a couple of calls, but only the easier jobs where they knew it wouldn't involve much physical work that would put a strain on his shoulder.

The team thought they were finished for the day, both Recker and Haley going home for the night. It was after nine when Jones asked them to come back. They rushed into the office again, knowing whatever it was, must have been urgent. Jones already had the information on the screen when they got here.

"This better be good," Recker said. "I got an angry look from someone when I said I had to come back in."

"You don't think I'd pull you back in this late at night for nothing, do you?" Jones replied.

"Well?"

Jones gave him an unappreciative glare before he proceeded. "It looks like we've got a job about to go down in..." Jones looked at the time. "Just about an hour."

"What's the stakes?" Haley asked.

"Clothing company on the boulevard."

"Boulevard's an easy target," Recker said. "Easy to get on and off in a matter of seconds and then you're gone a few minutes later before anyone knows what happened."

"Clothing company?" Haley asked, thinking it was a strange hit for thieves. "How much money could there be in that?"

"Depends if you're going for the cheap stuff," Recker said with a smile.

"Besides all that, this clothing company also sells fur coats," Jones replied. "Thousand dollars and up fur coats."

Haley whistled. "Man, expensive jawns, aren't they?"

Recker and Haley both turned and looked at him. "Jawns?" Jones said.

"What?" Haley asked. "They say that around here."

"We know. It's just that we've never heard you use that term before."

"Well, I figure I've been here long enough, might as well talk like a local."

Recker grinned. "Next thing you know he's gonna ask for a glass of wooder."

Haley smiled. "What makes you think I haven't already?"

Jones put his hands up to prevent the conversation from getting out of hand, as interesting as it may have been to discuss Haley's newfound vocabulary. Now wasn't the time for it. They had business to discuss, crimes to prevent.

"Anyway, so what's the score on this?" Recker asked.

Jones slightly shook his head. "As far as I can tell, we've got four or five perpetrators."

"Armed?"

"Heavily most likely. They have all done time for armed robbery. They have all been in and out of jail for most of their adult lives, which now spans about twenty years for each of them."

"So what you're saying is, when we find them, we can just pat them on the back and send them home to mommy?"

"Well, you could try, but I somehow think that would be... inappropriate."

Recker flexed his shoulder around. "Good thing this healed up when it did."

"Giving you any problems?"

"No, I'll be fine."

"What number would you give it? Percentage wise."

"Uh, I dunno, ninety-five, ninety-eight, something like that," Recker said.

"I suppose that's good enough."

"It'll have to be."

"Anyway, I intercepted some of their text messages, the last one was about half an hour ago. That was right before I called you two to come in. One of them asked if it was still on for tonight. The leader of the group confirmed that it was."

"And you're sure about the address?"

Jones glanced at him as if he couldn't believe that he was being questioned about the accuracy of his information. "Yes, I'm sure about the address."

"They been casing this place out do you know?" Haley asked.

"They don't need to."

"Why not?"

"One of the members of the group has been working there in the warehouse, loading trucks and whatnot. He's been there about three months."

"Probably picked there specifically for this moment," Recker said.

"Most likely."

"So four or five guys?"

"I've got four as a definite," Jones answered. "There's a fifth that I can't confirm will be there. It's possible he might just be the driver, but I can't say with certainty on that. I would probably count on him being there to be sure, then if he's not, then all the easier."

"But five's the max? No more than that."

Jones shook his head. "There's no evidence that I can see that indicates there's anyone else."

"So is that what they're after?" Haley asked. "The fur coats."

"Well, JB Clothing also has a number of other high end clothes. Expensive handbags that are three-four hundred dollars, hundred dollar jeans, five hundred dollar suits and dresses, things like that."

"So they could be after anything?"

"In one of the texts they mentioned furs specifically, but I wouldn't be surprised if they targeted other areas as well."

"Five guys, a lot of merchandise, they're probably gonna need a box truck or something," Recker said. "At least a van."

"I've already been checking that," Jones said. "There's been nothing rented or bought that I can see."

"Probably stole one."

"It's a good bet."

"You happen to know where all this merchandise is stored?"

"That I do not know. I've been checking plans, looking for pictures, checking websites, but I cannot get a read on where the merchandise is located."

"How big a building is it?" Haley asked.

"Two floors," Jones answered. "I would assume the first floor is where they keep everything and the second floor is office space like most are, but I cannot say for certain. So I can't say if all the clothes are grouped together or separated or however they have it laid out."

"How big's the building?" Recker asked.

"It's a large building. Whether it's one large open space or it's divided with walls into sections, I just can't say."

"If there's that much expensive merchandise in the building, they should have guards or something," Haley said. "At least a good alarm system."

"There is a security guard by a front gate. I assume he makes the rounds periodically. And I believe there is an alarm system as well. How they plan to do this I don't know."

"Probably plan on killing the guard," Recker said. "Get through the alarm system, take as much stuff as their truck will hold, then be off."

"Very well could be. In any case, you guys should get going. You're not going to have a lot of time to set up shop."

With under an hour to go before the supposed time

of the robbery, Recker and Haley quickly got their things together and rushed out of the office. It was close to a thirty-minute drive to get to the JB Clothing warehouse. That would give them just enough time to sneak in the building and wait for the crew to get there, hopefully surprising them during the act of the robbery. As they drove to the building, Recker and Haley discussed their plans.

"How are we gonna do this?" Haley asked.

"What do you mean?"

"Seems like that guard's gonna be in a lot of trouble no matter what. If we get into the building and wait for them, they could kill that guard while we're in there."

Recker sighed as he stared out the windshield. "Yeah."

As he drove, he tried to think of a way to keep the guard safe, while still protecting the building, as well as taking out the crew planning on robbing it. He wasn't coming up with many answers. If they took out the guard first upon getting there, making sure he was out of the way, but still safe somewhere, that could alert the crew that something was off and they could split before Recker and Haley had a chance at them. That could make them even more dangerous, making them communicate in a different way, or choosing a different building, or the same building, another night, another time, another day when Recker and Haley couldn't be there to combat them. Recker thought about one of them taking the guard's place, but that would put one of them in the line of fire too. And while he wasn't against putting himself in danger in place of someone else if he knew what was coming, the fact they didn't know how the crew was planning on getting in made the deal somewhat rougher.

Recker and Haley continued debating and throwing around different ideas, though they had yet to come up with a good one, one that would keep the guard out of harm's way. They thought of going straight up to the guard, telling him what the deal was, but that had its own risks. The guard could think they were lying, or trying to rob the place themselves, call the cops, or any number of other things that wouldn't have helped to protect him. They really had no concrete answers for what they wanted to do. But they weren't even sure the man's life was in danger either. The crew could have done just about anything with him. Beat him up, tied him up, knocked him out, stash him out of the way somewhere, they might have had anything in mind.

It would turn out to be a moot point, however. By the time Recker and Haley got to JB Clothing, they had gotten there too late. At least to help the guard. They initially drove by the gate, with Haley thinking he saw something.

"Turn around," Haley said.

"What's up?"

"Thought I saw something."

Recker looked at the time. "Can't be them yet. Should still have another thirty minutes."

"Maybe they can't tell time."

Recker swung the car around, taking a few extra minutes to turn around, then swing back the other way. Once they were within range of the warehouse, Recker slowed down, stopping just beyond the gate. Both men got out of the car and approached the gate.

"What'd you see?"

"Something that looked out of place," Haley answered.

Once they got to the gate, they both saw it. The guard was positioned up against the window of the guardhouse, his head leaning up against the glass. There was splotches of blood on the window, caused by the bullet going through the man's skull.

"Good eye by you," Recker said.

"I just noticed a bunch of stuff on the window as we drove by. Seemed odd that a guard station's windows wouldn't be clear."

"Well, guess we know what that was."

Haley looked at the guard and shook his head. "Guess we don't need to debate on what to do with him now."

Recker tapped his friend on the arm, not wanting them to get saddened over the man's death. There was nothing they could do for the guard now. But they could still deliver justice to the men that were responsible for it. Both men went to the gate and looked through it, observing a dark cargo van just outside one of the shipping doors. Recker put some strength into pushing the gate open, but it opened pretty easily.

"Good thing they didn't lock it," Haley said.

They quickly got through the gate, not opening it very far. Just enough for the two of them to squeeze through. They couldn't see if anyone was in the truck from that distance, and they didn't want to take the chance of them being seen coming through. Once on the inside, Recker and Haley clung to the wall, just watching for a minute. They didn't see any activity around the truck.

"They must be inside already," Recker said.

"How you wanna do this?"

"I don't wanna take a chance on being seen, especially if there is someone still in that truck." Recker looked around the property, observing the darkness around the edges of the fence. There wasn't much light there. "How about we each go a different direction? I'll go left, you go right. There's not much light by the fence, so we should be able to get there undetected in a couple minutes."

"Squeeze them off?"

"Yeah. We'll try to meet at the back of that truck and then surprise them inside."

"And if someone's in that thing?"

Recker shrugged, not seeing the issue. "Then take them out."

"Quietly I suppose?"

"That would be ideal."

Before moving out, they each checked their weapons again.

"You good?" Recker asked.

"Locked and loaded."

22

It only took a few minutes for both Recker and Haley to come up along the side of the building, using the darkness to help conceal their movements. Recker had the tougher task, having to get to the truck without having been seen, considering the truck was facing him. If someone was in it, and he still couldn't tell if there was from his vantage point, there would be no sneaking up on him. He stood there by the corner of the building, straining his eyes to see if there was someone in the truck. Haley was on the other side of the building, ready to go.

"I'm ready," Haley said. "What about you?"

Recker sighed, just not sure what he was dealing with. "I'm at the building. Just can't tell if someone's in that truck. If they are, they're being pretty still."

"Let me sneak around to the truck. I'll come up

alongside the door. If there's someone there, I'll take them out."

"All right, just be careful. I'll cover you from here if someone comes out of that building and spots you."

"Roger that."

Haley took a quick look to the building, making sure no one was coming, then sprinted from the corner of the building to the van, stopping just behind the bumper. He peeked around the tail light, looking in the side mirror, seeing an arm move by the steering wheel. Haley took three deep breaths, then hurried over to the driver side door. Once there, he immediately stuck his gun through the open window and let loose, firing two times, killing the driver instantly. The man slumped over across the seat, his head finding its final resting spot across the console.

"Driver eliminated," Haley said.

Upon hearing that, Recker also sprinted to the van, taking up a spot next to Haley along the door. They peeked through the window to the other side, and above the hood, waiting there for a minute to see if anyone was coming. Nobody was.

"You wanna just wait here for them?" Haley asked. "Can probably take them out as they come out."

"Unless they saw us and are going out the back way."

"Or they're just busy collecting everything. If I go around the back and cover the door, I might not be able to get in if it's locked and bolted. That's gonna leave you with four of them."

"Yeah. Assuming the driver's the fifth guy."

"Even if he's the fourth, that still leaves you with three."

"Let's just get closer and see what's inside," Recker said, not wanting to split up until he knew what was going on.

They ran around the edge of the van, going up to the building. They went up the five steps that led to the open door and went inside. The lights were on, so they could at least see what was in front of them. They walked down a short and narrow hallway, which split into two different directions. Recker took the left side, Haley took the right. They each walked past a couple of doors that were locked, with no lights on inside the rooms. They kept on going. Eventually, Haley's path led to another hallway, going to his left, which encompassed even more doors. It seemed as if that was the office part of the building. Recker's path quickly ended though, coming up to a door that led to the warehouse. He slowly opened it up and walked into the warehouse, standing by the closed door for a second as he sized up the situation. He didn't see anything at first. Then, he saw some boxes to his left that he could take cover behind, which he did.

"I'm in the warehouse," Recker said quietly.

"I'm still checking off doors," Haley replied. "Got anything?"

"Not yet. All quiet here. Don't hear anything. Anything on your end?"

"Nothing."

Recker stayed in his position for a moment, figuring something would break soon. If they were in the building somewhere, the crew would have to come to him, having to go in that direction to put the merchandise in the van. Knowing that, Recker didn't feel the need to have to go off and search for them. Especially if they were waiting for him, which might have been the case if they saw him coming or noticed what happened outside.

A few more minutes went by, and Recker was starting to get impatient. There was only so long he could stay in the same spot. He finally emerged from behind the boxes and started walking in the middle of the floor, no protection around him. He started walking toward the back of the warehouse. Then, he heard something that sounded like it was moving on some type of dolly or hand truck. Something that had wheels. Then he heard a bunch of voices, getting louder by the second. Recker started moving back to his original position, but he had already been spotted by that time.

"Who the hell's that?!" one of the crew yelled, pointing at him.

The other three men with him immediately opened fire at the strange man, Recker scurrying back to the boxes. He dove behind them, just as the boxes got lit up with bullets. Recker got down as low as possible, knowing that most people tended to shoot high. One thing was for sure, those boxes weren't providing much protection. They looked like swiss cheese now.

"Chris... found them!"

"I can hear! On my way!"

With the bullets coming in hot and heavy, Recker was pinned down, not really able to fire back. At least not safely. He was sure if he poked his head up then it would be shot off. He just had to hold on for another minute before his partner arrived. Haley ran down the hallway, running as fast as his legs would allow. Once he got to the door that led to the warehouse, he didn't stop to survey the situation, didn't slow down, didn't do anything that would delay him from helping out his friend. He barged through the wooden door, opening it up with his shoulder. He immediately flopped to the ground as he came in, seeing the suspects in front of him. Upon seeing a new guy there, Haley was now the one under fire. He quickly rolled to his right, seeing a bunch of boxes there, hoping to take cover.

Now that Haley was the target, Recker quickly popped up, knowing he had a short reprieve. He had to take advantage of it. He peeked out to the side of the boxes and took aim at the man to the left of the others. Recker fired, the man he was aiming for immediately dropping to the ground. He wasn't dead, though, and continued firing in Recker's direction. His bullets weren't really close to Recker though, his aim off by the shaking of his hand from being wounded so badly. Recker took aim at the injured man one more time, firing a fatal bullet that quickly put the man out of his misery.

Recker, wanting to move on from the bullet-ridden boxes he was currently behind, got to his feet, and made the decision to run to another spot. Hopefully, one where he could see the crew better. The crew they were up against were now splitting their focus. Two were still firing on Haley, who was keeping his head down until he got the opportunity to return fire. The other one turned on Recker, who stood up and sprinted from his spot, running about five feet to another set of boxes. This one had a few more to its stack.

Trying to avoid the bullets that were coming his way, Recker jumped head first over some of the boxes, landing hard on the injured shoulder of his that had just healed. He winced in pain and held it, feeling like the last few weeks of inactivity were now thrown out the window, meaningless. He muttered a curse word under his breath, taking a deep breath to get the pain out of his mind as he focused on the task at hand. Recker got down on the ground, lying on his stomach, and peeked around the corner of the stack he was behind. He figured it was the best spot. They'd be shooting at him like he was standing on his feet. Everyone aimed high. It never failed.

Recker took aim at another one of the men, firing

his gun at the man's chest. His aim must have been a little off from that position, since the man only grabbed his arm when he felt the bullet graze it. Recker looked at his gun like there was something wrong with it.

"I must be losing my touch."

All three men turned and started firing at Recker again, making him curl up on the ground as he waited for the bullets to stop. That provided the opportunity for Haley to rise up again, standing tall above the boxes. He took aim at the first man closest to him, the one Recker winged in the arm. A couple bullets to the chest later and the man no longer had to worry about his arm. Haley then took aim at the next guy, who had also fired at him simultaneously. With bullets hitting the boxes in front of him, and the concrete block wall behind him, Haley was undeterred, continuing to fire until he got his man.

With only one man remaining, the last surviving member of the crew was now scared for his life without the help of his buddies. Instead of continuing to fire, he ran off to the back of the warehouse. Haley started walking in that direction as well, not seeming to be in any hurry. He looked over at Recker's position to make sure he was OK. He saw Recker get back to his feet and brush himself off. Recker moved his shoulder around to make sure he still had a good range of motion.

"You all right?" Haley asked.

"Just landed hard on it. It'll be fine."

"Get hit?"

Recker shook his head. "Just on the floor."

"What do you wanna do with this guy?"

Recker sighed, wanting to be done with it. But they couldn't still leave one guy unaccounted for. Plus, he was part of the team that killed the guard. It wasn't like he was some innocent.

"I guess we should go get him."

"What if he gives himself up?" Haley asked.

Recker shrugged. "I dunno. Tie him up with a note for the police saying he killed the guard?"

"Works for me."

"We gotta find him first."

"Wonder if he slipped out the back?"

"Hope not. He's part of this crew which means if he did something like this once, he could do it again."

"Maybe we scared him straight?"

"How many times does that happen?"

"Once in a while."

"Maybe with some young kids who haven't been hardened yet," Recker said. "Not with experienced criminals who have a heavy package already."

Recker and Haley proceeded to walk to the back of the warehouse. They walked at a normal pace, like there was nothing urgent at hand. Their demeanor was cool and calm, like they hadn't just been in a small battle and killed three people. It was old hat to them. Once they got near the back of the warehouse, they saw the wall, and a door that hadn't been opened yet. They knew the last guy was still there, hiding somewhere. Recker pointed to his partner to split up again, each of them going wide to the edges of the wall, hoping they would find their target somewhere in the middle. Recker stopped for a moment, looking around at the hundreds of boxes that were littered around the floor. Some were big, some were small, some were stacked high, some were already on pallets, shrink-wrapped as they waited for a truck to take it to its retail destination. The last guy was there somewhere, perhaps waiting for a back to be turned to him, making it easier for him to escape.

"Give it up," Recker yelled. "Throw out your gun now and all you'll have to worry about is a prison sentence. You've done that before."

He waited a minute for an answer, but there was none coming. The man, still clutching his assault rifle, wasn't interested in pardons or giving himself up. He was getting out of there in one of two ways. Either walking out with the two guys chasing him dead, or him leaving in a body bag. That was it for him. He wasn't interested in anything else.

Recker continued moving forward, walking around some boxes, knowing that the man could jump out at him at any minute, at any turn. Eventually, he would. Recker looked around some more boxes, then froze in his spot for a moment, thinking he heard something. He didn't realize the man was coming up behind him, ready to take him out. The man moved a little closer to get a free and clear shot, raising his rifle to kill Recker with a shot to the back of the head. He squeezed the trigger, the bullet just missing Recker's head by inches. Recker ducked and turned, ready to fire. It wasn't necessary though. Haley saw the man and fired, milliseconds before the man was able to pull the trigger on Recker. The bullet from Haley entered the man's chest, just as he was firing on Recker. The force of the bullet entering his body was enough to throw his aim off as he fired, which was why he missed his shot on Recker. As the man fell to the ground, Recker went over to him, kicking the rifle further away from the dying man's body.

"Looked like you could use some help," Haley said with a grin.

Recker looked at him and nodded. "Mia would kiss you for that one."

"I would take it."

Recker went over to his partner and tapped him on the shoulder. "Let's get out of here."

"Another one wrapped up. Too bad about the guard, though."

Recker sighed, wishing they could have gotten there sooner to prevent the guard's death, even though he knew there was nothing they could have done. It wasn't their fault the crew got there early.

"Yeah. At least we got the men responsible for it though."

"I guess things should be getting back to normal now," Haley said.

"I don't know about that. There's still Naylor roaming around somewhere out there. Until he's neutralized for good, I don't think normal's in the cards."

23

The team was sitting around the office, taking one of the few breaks that they allowed themselves. Jones' software programs were still running, but there was nothing so pressing he needed to attach himself to. Recker and Haley were sitting on the couch, each having a soda, while Jones was on the microfiber chair, having a coffee. They were having one of those shoot-the-breeze moments, where they talked about anything that popped into their heads, no specific subject required. Most of it wasn't work-related. As Jones sipped on his coffee, he looked at Recker, wondering if he should say what had been on his mind for quite a while. He just never found the right time to ask. Or maybe he just never really wanted to ask, fearful of what the answer might be. Jones finally decided to just come out with it, since they were having a carefree session amongst each other.

"So have you decided when you're going to give this all up?"

Recker looked confused, taking the can from his lips and holding it with both hands on his lap. He looked at Haley, not sure how to respond. The question threw him for a loop.

"You wanna say that again?" Recker asked, wondering if maybe he'd been daydreaming and his friend actually asked a different question altogether.

"I was wondering if you had an idea about when you were going to walk away from all this?"

Now Recker knew he wasn't dreaming. The question still threw him for a loop though. It might have been the last question he ever would have suspected. "Um..." he shook his head, looking for an answer that wasn't so clear-cut. "I don't know. Haven't really given it that much thought. Why do you ask? Anxious to get rid of me?"

Jones laughed. "No, not quite. It's just... I know things with Mia have progressed..."

"I've been with Mia a few years now."

"I know, but... at some point... she's probably going to want you to make certain... lifestyle changes."

"Like a new profession?"

"I would be surprised if she didn't. You've been injured a few times now, you're getting older, I'm sure she doesn't want you to do this forever."

"Probably not. But I don't think I'm at the point where I have to decide that anytime soon. I think I still got a few more years in me. Is this your way of pushing me to the curb for younger blood?"

"Don't be silly."

"Have you identified another guy you'd like to bring in, put me out to pasture?"

"Now you're getting carried away. I simply asked an innocent question to get your thoughts on the matter."

"No ulterior motives?"

Jones shook his head. "No ulterior motives. Just trying to get inside your head a little bit."

"Careful... that's a dangerous place to be sometimes," Recker said with a smile.

"In all seriousness, you haven't given it much thought?"

Recker could see that his friend was genuinely interested in an answer. He tried to give him one the best that he could. "I guess I've thought about it. If I continue to do this, I can't see myself growing old in it. Eventually it would catch up to me, somewhere along the line. But I'm not ready to walk away. Not just yet."

"You will let me know when you are, right?"

"I would never leave you hanging or spring something on you. You know that. Why all the questions about it? What's this really about?"

"Oh, I don't know. I guess I've had thoughts of my own lately, about what I would do after all of this is over."

"You thinking about shutting it down?" Recker asked.

"No, not anytime soon. But living this life... it does take its toll. On the body, especially in your case, and in the mind. That's where it gets me the most. The constant problems, the constant danger, having to put you two into situations where I know you may not come back, the people you're helping that maybe can't be helped in time. It's been getting to me more and more lately."

"It's not easy."

"No, and it seems to be getting tougher all the time."

"Did we have a specific case or something that pushed you over the edge?"

"No. It's just the cumulative effect. I would suspect it happens in most professions, where you just get worn down and tired."

"Maybe you need a vacation."

"Perhaps so."

"Have you given thought to when you're gonna shut this down?"

Jones shook his head. "I would think when you guys have had enough, I probably will too."

"Where would you go after that?"

"I don't know." Jones looked at the window. "I think someplace warm. Maybe with some beaches. Maybe an island. Hawaii maybe. Or maybe one of those islands in the Caribbean."

"You guys are gonna go off and leave me by myself, huh?" Haley said

"No, like I said, I wouldn't be done with this until both of you are."

"What if I left tomorrow?" Recker said. "What would you do? Bring a new guy in?"

Jones thought for a minute. "No, I think we would just continue on with the two of us. It takes a lot of effort just to find and identify someone who would be suitable. And I'm not sure we would get lucky enough like we did with Chris, someone who could just blend right in without much of a problem. And then in five, ten years, whenever Chris would be done, then I would just turn the computers off and go live the rest of my life somewhere secluded."

"You think you could? Just turn the computers off like that? I know you. That's part of the reason why you sleep here instead of getting an apartment or something. You want to always be nearby in case something breaks."

"I would like to think I could. That I would. It might be more difficult than I make it sound, though. I have a feeling it would be easier for you than for us."

"Why's that?"

"It's always easier to walk away from something when you have something else to walk to."

"Mia?"

Jones nodded. "And she's definitely no consolation prize."

"There's nothing preventing either of you from

doing the same. Not necessarily even a woman, but something else that grabs you more."

"I doubt there would be something else. But I suppose it could never be discounted."

"One thing you always have to remember, David. This life we lead, we've done some good things, and we'll keep on doing them, and we've helped a lot of people, prevented a lot of people from getting hurt or killed. But with us here or with us gone, it'll never stop. The crime, the bad deeds, the bad people, all you do is switch the names, switch the faces, it'll never go away, no matter how much we do."

"I know. But if we're gone, how many more will get hurt if we weren't there to stop them?"

Recker looked at the wall briefly, remembering a conversation he once had with one of his CIA trainers. "When I was in the CIA, one of my mentors, he told me I would see a lot of bad things out there. Things I would never forget. He told me, you have to remember you're just one person out there. You can't stop every bad thing from happening in the world. You can do your part, do your share, prevent a lot of things, but you can't do it all alone. Everyone else has to do their share too."

Jones nodded, understanding what he was saying.

"Whenever we're all gone," Recker said. "Everyone else is going to have to do their share. We'll have done ours. And we should all be able to sleep at night knowing the job we did."

"I'll drink to that," Haley said, tapping their soda cans together.

"What about you?" Jones asked. "What are your thoughts about when this is over?"

Haley shook his head, not even able to think about such a time. "I don't know. That's gonna be no time soon, I can tell you that. I haven't been at this as long as you guys have, but I'm in no hurry to give it up anytime soon. Before coming here, my life was pretty much a wreck. Now I got a purpose. That's pretty much all anyone can ask for. I still got some years left in me. I'll probably still be doing this long after you guys hang them up."

"Why don't you start going out a bit more now?" Recker asked, looking at his original partner. "Go out, have a drink now and again, go on a date or two, this can't be your life forever. At least not all of it."

"I go out every now and then," Jones said.

"I'm not talking about the one time a month you come over for dinner with me and Mia. I'm talking about... like normal people. A couple times a week. Your software programs will still run, I'm sure you can set something up where you get an alert through your phone or smartwatch. You don't need to tie yourself to a chair in this room twenty-four hours a day."

"I suppose I've just gotten into that rut, afraid of the NSA finding me somehow, getting sloppy by being seen by some security camera somewhere."

"They're not looking for you anymore."

"Old habits die hard."

"Would you stay here when you're done?" Haley asked.

"I don't know," Recker replied. "This is as much of a home as I've ever had. Or as much as I've ever felt. And it's the only place Mia has ever known. But I am known here. Just living a normal life again might be hard to do. Maybe moving somewhere else would be the smart move. I dunno, we'll see. Hopefully I'll live long enough to get to make that call."

After a few more minutes of discussing their post-career plans, their discussion turned to things that were happening at the moment. Or at least the most recent past.

"Why do you think that Naylor never showed up at that warehouse with Vincent?" Jones asked.

"I've been stumped by that one myself," Haley replied. "I can't figure it."

Recker rubbed his chin as he thought. "Tough to say."

"Perhaps he got wind of the events somehow," Jones said. "Or maybe he suspected it might have been some type of setup?"

Recker quickly shot down that idea. "No, I don't think so. If he thought it was a setup, he wouldn't have sent in all those men. I mean, why would you? You wouldn't intentionally send in those guys if you thought there was a chance they weren't coming out."

"Unless he sent in so many believing they had

enough numbers to handle the setup," Haley said.

"Or maybe he really did have something else to do," Jones said. "Some other matter to attend to."

"What would be more important than killing me?" Recker asked.

Jones put his hand in the air and shook his head, not having an answer. "Unless he was setting something else up. I just can't understand it."

"How many men did we figure he had left?"

"Eight not including him."

"Enough to still do some damage."

"But not so many that we can't handle them all," Haley said.

"Sure wish I knew what they were planning next," Jones said.

"Be careful what you wish for," Recker replied. "You know what they say to that."

"Yes, but I wish I knew whether they were planning some type of payback, or whether they were recruiting, or something else entirely."

"Maybe all of the above."

"Or that."

"It's been two weeks since anyone has seen or heard from them," Haley said. "Maybe they really got the message."

"That I think is wishful thinking," Jones replied.

"I think one thing we can count on," Recker said. "Is that it won't be long before we hear from them again."

24

nother week went by, and the team felt like things were getting back to normal without having to worry about the Scorpions. It wasn't that they felt the group was gone for good, they fully expected to have to deal with them again at some point, but it did seem like they had flown the coop. Recker and Haley had no contact with them, or with Vincent's crew, and simply were handling their own business, one job at a time. And a busy time it was. It seemed that business had really picked up in the last week.

Whether it was just a coincidence, or whether the Scorpions being run out of town somehow had an aftereffect and made the other criminals in town go crazy, Recker and Haley felt like they were constantly running around. There were no off days, no taking it easy at night, or in the morning for that matter. It seemed the whole city had gone nuts.

Recker and Haley had rarely worked together in the past week. With so many things going on, they were usually off on their own, barely bumping into each other. They had both gotten back to the office at relatively the same time, though on this occasion, Haley beat his partner in by about thirty minutes. Haley was sitting down having a drink when Recker walked in.

"Hey stranger," Haley said. "Long time no see."

Recker smiled, looking weary. All he could manage in reply was a simple little wave. "Hey yourself."

"You two look like you could use a good stiff drink," Jones said.

"I would if I thought I could get twenty minutes to enjoy it."

Recker sat down in a chair. He leaned back and closed his eyes. Within a few minutes, he drifted off to sleep. It was a short-lived rest, however, as his phone rang, waking him up.

"No rest for the weary," Recker said, picking up his phone. He saw it was Vincent calling, and he hung his head. He really didn't have the time or inclination to go to one of their meetings now. Or tomorrow either probably. "Oh, no."

"Bad news?" Jones asked.

"I don't know if I feel like finding out." Recker contemplated just letting it go to voicemail, or calling

Vincent back later, but he felt kind of bad blowing him off like that. Especially after he helped clear out some of the Scorpions a few weeks back. He reluctantly answered. "Yeah?"

"Mike, glad I got you. I need your help and I need it now."

Recker immediately perked up, sitting up straight. Jones and Haley saw from the look of concern on their partner's face that something wasn't right.

"What's wrong?" Recker asked.

"I'm in danger. Naylor and the rest of his men have cornered me off."

"Where's Malloy and the rest of your boys?"

"Jimmy's here with me. The rest... they've been killed."

"What happened?"

"An ambush. We walked right into one. I'd love to tell you the rest of the story sometime, but right now, we could really use some assistance."

"Where are you at?"

"Down near the airport."

"The airport?! Jeez, that's gonna take us some time to get down there."

"I know. We'll try to hold off as long as we can."

"What about the rest of your men?" Recker asked.

"Can't get a hold of them yet."

"OK, we're coming. Just hold on. Where are you at specifically?"

"Past the airport, take the Industrial Highway, then

when you get to Saville, take a left at the light. Go down to Second Street, take a left. There's a big white building on the right. There's a small gate in the front with an American flag waving above it. We're in there."

Recker sighed, knowing that was a little bit of a hike from where they were. "We'll do what we can, but that's a little ways out. It's gonna take us at least thirty minutes to get there and that's pushing it."

"Anything you can do I'd appreciate."

"Can you hold out that long?"

"We'll certainly do our best."

"We're on the way." Recker put his phone away and sprung out of the chair. He looked at his partner as he rushed to the gun cabinet. "C'mon, we gotta load up and go."

Haley went over and the two of them quickly geared up. "What's going on?"

"Vincent and Malloy are pinned down by Naylor and the rest of the Scorpions. They're half an hour away."

Jones cleared his throat and was about to say something. Recker put a stop to that.

"Don't have time for bickering now, David. We gotta go."

"I understand that," Jones said. "I wasn't going to argue."

Recker and Haley continued getting ready, grabbing everything they needed, along with some extra stuff in case the standoff lasted a while. They were ready to go in just over a few minutes.

"I was just going to say... be careful," Jones said.

Recker and Haley scurried to the door. Recker looked back at his partner before leaving. "Always are."

Jones laughed to himself as he watched them close the door, disappearing into the night. "Always indeed."

Recker and Haley jumped in their car and raced out of the parking lot, pushing the speed limit, along with a few yellow lights, until they got to I-95. Recker was driving, and he gunned it the entire length of the highway, going about ten miles per hour over the speed limit, making sure he wasn't going too fast to avoid any State Troopers that were lined up along the highway. They couldn't give Vincent and Malloy any help if they were getting stopped for speeding.

Once they got near the airport, Recker called Vincent, to make sure they were still hanging in there. He also wanted to see what they were walking into. It took a few rings, but Vincent eventually picked up.

"We're about ten minutes out," Recker said.

"Can't come fast enough," Vincent replied.

"What's the situation?"

"It's me and Jimmy, and there's about six of them. We knocked two of them off."

"How are you guys on ammo?"

"Uh, we're pushing our limits. Honestly don't know if we've got enough to last until you get here."

"What's the layout of the building?"

"Once you get over the fence, there's a main entrance. Go past that until you get to the side door. It's white. It's also open. Once you come in, there's a big open area. Go past that until you go down a long narrow hallway. Once you get to the end of that, there's a glass door. Go through that and that's where we are. We're to the right in the back corner. They're spread throughout the room."

"Get a hold of any of your other men?"

"Yes, but they won't get here until after you."

"OK. We're coming."

Once Recker turned off the Industrial Highway, he sped down Saville, then squealed his tires as he turned onto Second. He raced down the street, not even thinking about whether the Scorpions had a lookout posted. Once the SUV came to a screeching halt, Recker and Haley jumped out of the car and ran towards the small chain-link fence. It was half the normal size of a regular fence, so the two men had no trouble in jumping over it.

They instantly saw the main doors that Vincent had told them about and ran toward the side of the building. Luckily for them, there were no Scorpions out in front, waiting for intruders. That would have given their surprise appearance away instantly. Once Recker and Haley got to the side door, they slowly opened it, not sure what they would find inside. It had been ten minutes since they talked with Vincent. A lot could change in ten minutes. Especially when guns were involved.

Recker and Haley stepped inside the building. Just as Vincent had told them, it was empty. And quiet. Too quiet for all that was supposed to be happening. Even if the battle was in another room, they still should have been able to hear gunfire. It was eerily silent though. It was that weird kind of silence, the kind after a battle has ensued, and it's the few minutes after, when it seems like guns should still be firing, even though there's nothing left to fire at.

They were standing in a large room, but there weren't a whole lot of obstacles to look around. It was pretty vacant except for a few loosely thrown boxes here or there. Nothing they couldn't look over though. And certainly nothing anyone would be stupid enough to hide behind. They quickly ran over to the hallway, just as long and narrow as Vincent had described. They passed by several doors, though for once, they didn't pay much attention to them. They were only focused on getting to that other door, and what was beyond it.

Once they got to the glass door, they tried to look through it, though it wasn't easy. It was clear, more of the stained type. They could see a few bodies moving, but it was more of a blur. As they listened at the door, they could hear a voice talking. He was calm, rational, talking in a slow manner. It didn't seem to suit the occasion. Without knowing exactly what they were walking into, they listened at the door for another minute, not wanting to rush in blind, though they knew it was likely they would have to at some point.

Naylor was walking around his two captives, both of whom were kneeling on the floor with their hands behind their heads. There were Scorpions standing all around Vincent and Malloy, guns in their hands, though not pointed at the two prisoners.

"It's a shame it had to come down to this," Naylor said. "We could have been great partners."

Vincent laughed. "Who are you kidding? This was always in your plans. My actions a few weeks ago just speeded up the process. You were so concerned with The Silencer that you put me on the back burner. But let's not kid ourselves now, huh? Your plan was always to take me out."

Naylor smiled. "Yeah, I guess it was. I had always thought it was going to be much more grander than this though. A car explosion, something big and... boomy. This is kind of... a little on the disappointing side. You getting shot, execution style, doesn't quite have the same effect."

"I'm sure you'll move on with your life just as easily with a boring shooting."

"If you wanna make it more interesting, give me a gun and we'll see what happens," Malloy said.

Naylor laughed. "Entertaining to the end. The right hand muscled up idiot."

Recker nodded at Haley, making sure he was ready. Rifles in hand, Recker threw open the door, him and

Haley rushing inside. Recker threw himself down to the ground, immediately lighting up the first man he saw. Haley went in and dropped to a knee, drilling the closest guy to him. As the Scorpions were confused as to what was going on, Malloy took advantage of the opportunity and punched the man behind him in the private parts, stealing the man's weapon as he dropped to the ground in pain. He then put a few holes in the man's chest as he looked for his next victim. Recker and Haley both took down another man each as the bullets flew over their heads. Malloy took care of another guy, drilling him in the back as he was shooting at the others.

Suddenly, all the gunfire stopped. The rest of the Scorpions were gone. All except for one. Naylor dropped his gun and put his hands in the air. He knew there was nothing to be gained for continuing the battle. It was lost. Recker and Haley each got back to their feet, though Recker was holding his shoulder again, hitting the ground hard once more. Haley looked over at his partner, seeing him wince.

"You good?"

Recker sighed. "Yeah."

"Gentlemen," Naylor said. "I'm sure we can come to some type of agreement. Let me go and I swear I'll never step foot in this city again."

Vincent stood behind the Scorpion leader and put the pistol that Naylor had dropped to the back of his head. He pulled the trigger, Naylor instantly dropping to the ground from the bullet that penetrated his skull. "No, I don't think you will."

Recker and Haley stared at Vincent, a look of surprise on their faces. It was the first time they had ever seen Vincent commit an act of murder. Or any act for that matter. Vincent looked down at Naylor and dropped the gun, wiping his hands with a handkerchief. Vincent then looked at his saviors.

"What? You thought I was incapable? You thought I got to this position by talking myself into it?"

"Not at all," Recker answered.

"Sometimes you have to get your hands dirty."

"I agree. So how'd all this get started?"

Vincent put his hand in the air, not really wanting to get into it. "Ahh, suffice it to say, I had a business deal lined up, the people I thought I was dealing with never showed, these other people opened fire on us and killed five of my guys, leaving me and Jimmy to fight for ourselves."

"So how'd you get into that little situation when we walked in?"

"Well, you recall I told you we were running out of ammunition?"

"Yeah."

"That's what happened. I knew you were coming soon. I just had to keep them talking long enough until you got here." Vincent then laughed. "Though I was beginning to run out of things to say."

Recker smiled. "I think I already know the answer to all this, but you need any help cleaning all this up?"

Vincent shook his head. "No. We got it. But thanks for the help. Remind me I owe you lunch the next time we meet."

Recker grinned and nodded. "I'll remember."

Recker and Haley bid the two men goodbye, then left the building. As they walked back to the car, Haley inquired again about his friend's shoulder, seeing that it was causing Recker some pain.

"You wanna tell me the truth about that shoulder now?"

Recker put his hand on the shoulder, having trouble moving it around. "Well, I think I'm gonna get another extended vacation."

ABOUT THE AUTHOR

Mike Ryan lives in Pennsylvania with his wife, and four kids. Visit Mike's website at www.mikeryanbooks.com to find out more about his books, and sign up for his newsletter to be notified of new releases.

 facebook.com/mikeryanauthor

instagram.com/mikeryanauthor

ALSO BY MIKE RYAN

The Eliminator Series

The Cain Series

The Extractor Series

The Ghost Series

The Brandon Hall Series

The Last Job

A Dangerous Man

The Crew

CPSIA information can be obtained
at www.ICGtesting.com
Printed in the USA
LVHW020052080921
697225LV00012B/246

9 798705 710195